THE
DREAM
PROPHETS
OF MISTLETOE

THE DREAM PROPHETS

OF MISTLETOE

BOGART NOMAD

SHOCKAHIKU

PRODUCTIONS

ISBN: 978-0-5788137-3-8 (Paperback)

Cover artwork by Opie Otterstad (Opieart.com)

SHOCKAHIKU
PRODUCTIONS

Printed in the United States of America

10 9 8 7 6 5 4 3 2 1

For "Umpsie"

CONTENTS

Flying over a wind-blown cornfield. The stalks are high and full.
A high-rise apartment building forty stories high; the clouds fly past in
the opposite direction.
A burning bush in a courtyard
A girl with purple feathers in her hair
Cables and chords snake their way to a table.
Blinding light
A whispered voice: Do not be afraid.

Dominix wakes up; he always wakes up just as the voice whispers in his brain and in his dream. He is annoyed and still tired. He rolls over and falls back to sleep. He hears the elevated train pulling into Lake Street Station.

Bluford Foot is riding the Woodlawn Lake elevated train into work, and his first stop of the day for the Mistletoe Delivery Service. He has his transistor radio on low enough to not disturb anyone. He has a single earpiece so he can hear the countdown from the local radio station, KTOE. The lady on his non-earpiece side is intently leaning in to listen. The DJ comes on after a song.

That was "Everybody Plays a Fool" by the Main Ingredient at No. 39. We are just getting started with Big Willy's Sunday Countdown of MY favorite forty songs from this past week. At No. 38, "Wildflower by Skylark ...."

Bluford is running a bit late. Reading the leftover sports section left behind by a factory lady, he smiles to himself and ponders a stray thought of just how blessed his life has turned out. It is the first day of

July 1973. Summer vacation for the school kids is in full swing, and it's the Founders Day parade this afternoon and festivities until dawn. It is a high holiday for the town of Mistletoe, Texas.

Bluford exits and feels like singing the tune he heard on the radio. He walks down the platform stairs and under the station, handing off the sports section to one of the retirees on the corner by the diner.

"Hey Lou," he says with a smile. Lou waves but keeps gesturing a story to two buddies at a table outside the Lake Street Cafe.

"Hey Blufoot," says the man next to Lou.

Bluford listens to Lou until the punch line, laughs authentically, then heads into the cafe before his shift to pick up two glazed blue donuts. He drops a single Nation of Texas Silver Dollar onto the counter, letting it clang out. It is a healthy tip for his favorite waitress. He is halfway out the door before he hears a cheerful "thank you" from behind the coffee pot area.

Across the street from the diner, he unlocks the door and clocks into his Mistletoe Delivery Service refrigerated shed and inspects his MDS cart. Chilled milk, eggs, and newspapers are securely in their appointed places and cubby holes. The late-night shift has done their job. Bluford checks his morning delivery list. There are two new welcome baskets for arrivals on his first stop: Mistletoe Street, the oldest street in town. Each basket is festively adorned with fruits, veggies, flowers, and brochures of upcoming Mistletoe events. The brochures are extra, just in case they were left behind at the depot during registration.

Bluford's uniform is complete except for his delivery hat. He begrudgingly takes off his O'Cherokee's championship hat fresh from an NBA finals victory just four weeks before. He has no problem with the standard Mistletoe delivery hat. He likes hats, but he is still chest crested, full of pride for his Valliant Cherokee Nation and their hard-fought seven-game final's series. He hangs the championship hat in his locker and finishes off his crisp clean uniform for the day's journey replete with his MDS top hat. He walks out of the shed, locks the door, and takes a sharp right turn on the sidewalk to make his first daily stop at the next corner.

His first stop is at 2102 W. Mistletoe Street.

Grandma Maxwell is sitting on the front porch of her New Orleans French Quarter–style two-story home on the corner of Lake and Mistletoe. She is reposing with a casual, closed-eye smile, basking in the sun of a new day before the heat overcomes her breath and she must retreat indoors. There is a rainbow-haired cat curled up in her lap. She rocks in her old wooden chair like a sea captain in the middle of the ocean, her mind drifting back to the Caribbean, the Gulf, or just down a lazy Texas river. Tulpen, the long-haired purring vessel, likes a firm hand to stroke her long, colorful body. Grandma is content to hold her close and feel her motorboat at her fingertips. Cat and human both breathe in deeply the sudden breeze that comes upon them just before being interrupted.

"Hello, Miz Maxwell." Bluford says ascending the porch steps with her carton of eggs.

Grandma does not flinch. She feels his presence. She finishes her deep breath of breeze, opens her eyes, and smiles wide. In her thick southern accent, she thanks her delivery man. " Much obliged, Mr. Foot." She pauses to take in his joyous demeanor. "I see you are still glowing like a Texas sunset. What's got you so blessed with contentment today!"

"Still enjoying the lad's victory from O'Cherokee, maam!" he states proudly.

"Oh, my Lord, those basketball boys made me proud as well." She rises up in her chair and clasps her hands together as if to pray and gently claps appreciation for her friend.

At this point Tulpen raises up her back and stretches. She turns and wrinkles her nose at Grandma and carefully jumps down as if it were a bit much on her old legs. She saunters slowly off the porch and down the stairs as the two friends continue their talk of sports pride and commiseration.

Tulpen then heads down the slight hill that is the end of the block and crosses the street to 2103. This nine-house stretch of street is the oldest part of the grand experiment of a town called Mistletoe, Texas.

The cat stays on the sidewalk headed for the treehouse at the end of the short block. She has a nice warm pillow in the treehouse calling her name.

She enjoys Grandma Maxwell's lap when it is undisturbed, but she is not in the mood for listening to a festive conversation. She has been half-heartedly carousing all night and is ready for bed. The treehouse is her home. Dom claims her as his, but she belongs to this block. She notices three bicycles strewn about the base of the treehouse and remembers that the boys had their weekend sleepover.

Tulpen hears a noise behind her. She stops and slowly turns around to see the source of the noise. An MDS delivery carriage wagon has sauntered upon her street. The heavy-duty golf cart at the head of this caravan slowly heads straight for her and house No. 2105. She darts off the cobblestone path and into the base of a palm tree in front of No. 2107 where Dom lives with his twin brother and family. She crouches down to watch. She has seen moving day for new residents before, but the carriages keep coming—on both sides of the street! She sees Bluford hurrying to greet the new families with their welcome baskets as they disembark. Someone is moving into No. 2104 also! Tulpen waits for a distraction so as not to be seen, then heads for the treehouse.

At the base of this massive structure of a clubhouse, Tulpen pauses to see the new neighbors, trying to pick them out from the bevy of MDS delivery people. The fourth carriage is filled with people instead of boxes, and sure enough, when it stops, kids and adults scurry off the back. She notices three dogs on leashes and at least one cat carrier held by a young girl with long, black hair. The black-haired girl lags behind the others, caring for her precious cargo. She has bright purple feathers in her hair. That is odd for a human, she thinks to herself. Tulpen hopes to get a glimpse of what must surely be another cat inside the carrier. Just as she fixes her gaze intently, the girl stops and quickly spins around and looks right at Tulpen from across the block.

Stacy Stone locks eyes with Tulpen and smiles knowingly. Stacy then looks down at her cargo in the carrier. She opens the small gate door and a black-and-purple cat peeks out but does not leave the carrier. Stacy looks at her cat and then back at Tulpen. She closes the gate just as another child walks up to her. He looks about the same age. Chad Simms stands beside Stacy and looks toward Tulpen with an expressionless face. Stacy whispers something to him, and they walk into No. 2104 and don't look back.

Tulpen turns and heads up the tree using the 2 x 4 wooden board steps to climb up into the structure perched fifteen feet above the ground. The sturdy sycamore tree holds two structures built by the kids of this block. One of the dads helped them with all the hard parts. The main clubhouse is just big enough to hold six sleeping bags. Up another ladder and ten more feet up from the pentagon-shaped box is another smaller wooden box that looks more like the crow's nest of a ship. Tulpen peeks her head into the first level, and she sees four sleeping bags and the gentle, heavy sleep-breathing of three ten-year-old boys. She tiptoes around the lumps, surveying which one she wants to wake up first. Next to a half-eaten bag of chips is a red sleeping bag.

One arm is flopped out, and Tulpen notices that Rich Mistletoe is flat on his back, sprawled closest to the entrance. His head is half on his pillow and half off. Tulpen decides to let him sleep. She moves past him and over to a drab green, old army surplus sleeping bag that looks very uncomfortable. Sleeping on his belly and nearly snoring is Izaak Black. Izaak is Rich's unofficial brother. Izaak's dad has raised Rich as his own just outside the Grand Mistletoe Mansion that is at the end of this block, just sideways over from this sycamore tree. Rich and Izaak grew up together with Izaak's sister Cecilia. Their dad is head groundskeeper and caretaker for this block. He has worked for the Mistletoe family all of his life, and his kids have been unofficial siblings to Rich, the bastard child of the Mistletoe hierarchy.

Tulpen remembers from previous awakenings that Izaak can lash out when awakened unexpectedly. She heads over to the last occupied bag in the far corner from the opening. Dominix Blue is stirring.

"Do not be afraid. Do not be afraid," he whispers.

He rubs his eyes and senses Tulpen is near. His head bolts up as he sees Tulpen. He makes a strange noise with his mouth. It's like someone trying to sound like a bat whispering. It is the noise he uses to call for Tulpen. She sits back on her haunches and looks out the window toward the moving carriages.

"Come here girl; say hello." Dom gestures to the cat. She turns and looks at him, blinks, and looks back out the window.

"Playing hard to get?" he asks.

THE DREAM PROPHETS OF MISTLETOE | 6

Tulpen sighs. *Humans don't get the hint,* she thinks to herself.

"I had that dream again, Tulpen." Dom looks at the cat, hoping for a response. He gets none.

"It's like a church dream; maybe I should ask Pastor about it after services." Tulpen keeps looking out the window. Her crystal-beaded collar catches some of the sunlight, and it beams a small laser of light onto Dom's face.

There is a loud noise from the movers, and Dom hears it. Izaak stirs, then rolls over onto his side, nearly on top of Rich. Dom sits up and crawls over to Tulpen by the window. He looks out, then crouches down to peek, so as not to be seen. The two new families are outside and in the street, surveying their new surroundings.

Dom shakes Izaak's leg and hollers in a whispered urgent tone, "Guys wake up. We got new neighbors."

Izaak jumps and bonks his head on the milk crate full of comic books. "Owww, crappers!" he bellows out. Dom jumps on him covering his mouth with his hand. Izaak is now on his back. His eyes are wide open and wondering what is going on. Rich doesn't even stir.

Dom brings a single finger up to his lips, "Shhh."

He lets Izaak up and motions to the window, "New neighbors?" he says.

"Which house?" Izaak whispers back.

"Both!" Dom shoots back.

"No way," Rich chimes in. Now awake, he is struggling to sit up and get his bearings.

All three sneak over to the window and look out at all the commotion.

The Simms family is moving into No. 2105.

No. 2105 is a spread-out, one-story in the style of a Mexican villa with a cool garden courtyard in the direct center of the house. It easily takes up the entire 2105 lot next to Dom's house at 2107. Across the street, the Stone family moved into 2104, next to Grandma Maxwell's New Orleans French Quarter–style home. 2104 is the coolest-looking house on the block. It is a seven-pointed, multilevel A-frame style home. The previous owner was kind of spooky. No one has ever seen the inside of 2104.

"How many kids you count so far?" Izaak asks the other two.

Many youngsters are running around with the now-unleashed dogs. The A Frame has a fenced-in yard, and they see the gate is open. All six of the kids are now trying to round up all the excited canines.

"I got five," Rich says quietly. He is guessing. His eyes are trained on the girl with the long hair and feathers. She is wearing a skirt in this morning heat!

"Nope, I got six," Izaak says certainly and quietly. "I see three boys and three girls. One of the girls is in a dress!" Then he pauses and counts out loud, "One, two, three dogs." He looks at the others from behind his binoculars. He smiles like Tulpen.

"Hey guys, why are we whispering?" Dom asks.

They all three look at each other and sit back on the floor around their bags. They ponder the question for a longer period than necessary.

Rich breaks the thought, "Hey, Where's Zoltar?"

Dom ignores Rich's question, "What are the odds that both houses get new people on the same day?"

"Yeah, that's kinda cool," Izaak ponders, "but freaky weird too."

Rich is looking through Zoltar's empty bag as if the large boy would be hiding inside of it.

"I bet they know each other … that happened over on Summit Street," Dom says with authority.

Tulpen crawls into Dom's lap, demanding attention.

"One thing is for certain, with that many new kids …" Dom starts to say before interrupted by Izaak.

"Six kids!"

"Six kids, yes … the kids on the block won't be the same," Dom says.

"We need a better name for our group than that," Izaak states.

A loud voice from the newness calls out, "Hey there's a basketball hoop!" One of the boys from 2105 comes over to check it out.

The hoop is right next to the sycamore treehouse at the end of the block.

He runs over, jumps up to try and touch the chain-link net. He comes close. He lands triumphantly and looks around for a ball. Finding none, he turns and runs back to his new house.

Izaak reaches over and collects his ABA ball and clutches it into his chest. "Yeah, things are gonna change." He sighs.

The boys each sit quietly for a moment wondering just exactly what will change now that their space has been invaded.

"Should we go say hi?" Izaak asks the other two.

"Eventually," Dom says quickly, "First things first. What time is it? We need to get to Pinkys and get the new Super Tribal Nation edition No. 43."

Izaak shoots the ball into the corner, swishing the comic book milk crate, "Comics, yes, it is Comic Book Sunday!"

Dom looks at Rich who is about to speak.

"And we need to find Zoltar."

Rich points at him aware but still half groggy. "I need a Dr. Pepper," Rich says, realizing he is actually newly awakened.

The sound of baseball cards in bicycle spokes draws closer and closer. The boys look down the hole to the base of the tree. The girls have arrived.

The rest of this block's little tribe pull up on their ten-year-old rides. Sasha Looks-Twice Quinterro is first, always in the lead. She lays down her bike and stands defiantly with hands on her hips. She surveys what the boys have seen.

She turns to her main sidekick, Cecilia. "New neighbors," Sasha says with an unknown purpose.

Izabella DaVinci and Wu Punabi pull up on their bikes but stay on them. They are not to be bothered by change. Wu fiddles with her handlebar basket. Izzy could care less and just stares at the scene.

Sasha calls up to the boys, "Ya'll seeing this?" There is no response.

"Hey Dipsticks! You morons awake up there?"

Izaak is already crawling down the ladder.

Rich starts down through the entrance hole. "Pipe down big mouth, we're awake," sounding perturbed. "Hold your horses; we see 'em."

"Ya'll didn't forget what today is, did ya!" Sasha says bluntly like a VSC drill sergeant.

"Duh!" Izaak jumps off the ladder and says in Sasha's face.

"Founders Day."

"What number is Big Willy up to?" Izzy asks Cecilia, oblivious to the commotion.

Cecilia has a portable transistor radio sitting in the straw basket attached to Wu's handlebars. She turns the volume back up. A song is just finishing.

They all stop to listen.

No. 24 on our weekly countdown is from Dr. John with the existential pondering of right places and wrong times. We know what time it is, don't we folks?

DJ Big Willy of radio station KTOE pauses.

There is dead air on the radio, waiting for someone to respond to the question. A small voice comes on. The group gets closer to Cecilia who is now holding the radio up for all to hear. She calmly grimaces at the personal space invasion.

"A commercial?"

A small child's voice says a second time but louder.

"Yes, little lady,"

Big Willy bellows.

"What is your name again, my petite little rocker?"

The gang draws even closer to Cecilia and her transistor.

"Back up!" she complains.

"Jessica Little Flower"

says the small voice.

"And how old are you?"

Big Willy asks a little more calmly this time.

"8, and a half"

"Fantastic, Thanks Miss Little Flower, we do need to hear from our sponsors, but first I just cannot resist turning up this next song! No. 23 on this week's countdown of Big Willy's favorite songs. They're not all new."

The group finishes the catchphrase together …

"But they all rock!" they all shout in unison.

The very catchy guitar chord of Deep Purple's "Smoke on the Water" kicks in, and Dom reaches over Sasha to turn up Cecilia's transistor.

"We gotta get down to the General Store! No. 20 is always a request! I want to get there and put in a Partridge Family song," Cecilia says very demandingly.

"You heard her, boys, mount those Schwinn knockoffs, and let's ride," Sasha says to rally everybody.

Dom teases Cecilia as she gets moving, "Danny Partridge and Cecilia, sitting in a tree … K I S S I N G!"

"Keith, I love Keith; Danny Partridge can kiss my ass," Cecilia yells at Dom at the top of her lungs.

Most of the two new families stop what they are doing and look over to the bike-riding gang.

Izzy sheepishly waves to them, mouthing the word "Hi."

Rich picks up his bike and asks Sasha, "You seen Zoltar?"

She shakes her head no.

Rich lets the others head toward the bridge that goes over the creek and into the playground of the school. Pinky's General Store is four blocks worth of land away from this spot. They will travel through the elementary school and the middle school playgrounds and lunch area. Rich looks back to catch a glimpse of Stacy Stone. He is smitten. At that very moment, his stomach jumps, and he could swear years later that he entered puberty at that very moment. *She's beautiful,* he thinks to himself and gently says it out loud in a whisper only Tulpen can hear. She meows at him from above, recognizing the moment.

Dom calls back from his green metallic banana seater with the gorilla handlebars. "Richard Mistletoe! Let's go."

Tulpen watches them ride off. She feels safe now. Maybe, safer than she has ever felt in over fifty years. She stretches her wings out and then pulls them back to her body and tucks them out of sight. She curls up under the window on the pillow Dom has left for her.

2

PINKY CLIFFORD'S MERCANTILE

Dom and Izaak are hovered over their favorite titles in the middle of the comic book racks of the general store. They are searching for the Silver Surfer-Crazy Horse crossover edition, No. 14. It is very rare.

Rich and Sasha are in the Music section, thumbing through the vinyl albums. Rich is looking for an Elton John album he heard Big Willy talk about. Sasha is next to him, acting like she cares. She keeps staring over at Dom as he excitedly looks through the racks.

"Hey, what did ya'll talk about last night? Stay up late?" she asks Rich while standing close so no one else can hear.

An interrupted Rich stops and looks her back a few inches to a proper personal space distance.

She scooches over.

"No seriously, did ya'll talk about us girls?" Sasha presses.

Rich didn't say anything.

"You know, who's cutest, who's ..."

Rich cut her off. "Well, little Miss Nosey, Dom didn't talk about you at all," he says bluntly and knowingly.

"Not even a little?" Sasha asks again.

"Nope" Rich states decidedly, quashing all hopes of Sasha learning anything new about her boy crush.

"Found it!" Rich says happily.

Sasha grabs it and reads the title out loud, *"Tumbleweed Connection?"*

"Yup, Big Willy mentioned it a few weeks ago. I asked Pinky to order it for me." Rich takes it back and adds it to his other albums. The speakers above them crackled with the radio.

And now at No. 20, we have a request from a veteran listener, Cecilia Black, this goes out to you. "I think I love you" by the Partridge Family."

Big Willy holds up a picture to the glass wall of the booth. It is an 8 x 10 color glossy of Keith Partridge.

Sasha and Rich look over to the sound booth in the back corner of the music section and see Cecilia and a few other Countdown Kids, jumping around outside Big Willy's booth.

"Cecilia and Danny sittin in a tree …" Dom hollers loudly from across the room.

"Shut up, Dom!" Cecilia screams at him before he can sing another word.

Rich moves into the K section, "So you really, like Dom, or what?"

Rich says without even making eye contact with Sasha.

Sasha begins to turn red, which pisses her off. She crosses her arms and sighs loudly, tripped up by her real feelings.

"Don't worry; I will not embarrass you," Rich says calmly hoping to gain her trust on the matter.

He stops at a Kinks album and looks at her, showing her the album cover, saying, "They spelled *Conspiracy* wrong."

She calms down a bit.

"Tell ya a secret," he says to Sasha to change her mood.

She looks at him, "Yeah?"

"I think I fell in love with that new girl we just saw back on the block," he says to her confidentially.

Sasha has a big open mouth and then pauses, sensing a real moment from Rich—that is nothing to tease about.

He looks back at her, knowing he just exposed his feelings to her.

Sasha uncrosses her arms and puts a hand on his shoulder. Then she says assuredly, "My dad says we can't fall in love at age ten. Our hormones haven't kicked in yet … well, not for boys at least," she says waiting for a response.

Rich is thinking. Then he says, "Does Keith Partridge count as love?"

She looks at him, not knowing if he is serious or not. Sasha wants to be a teacher and is learning when teaching moments happen or is someone screwing around with her.

"You know girls mature faster than boys!" Sasha says in that all-knowing manner that Rich has heard often.

Rich rolls his eyes. He moves on to the L section.

Sasha scooches next to him and whispers, "I tell ya what, I will do some snooping on the new girl as long as you bring up my name to Dom. But be all cool-like, when you do it."

"Deal," Rich says very assuredly.

There is a big pause. Sasha acts like she is looking at records but is really watching Dom from afar.

Rich then speaks up, "So now that I am all mature and in love like a girl, do I have to hang out with you, Cecilia, Izzy, and Wu at your tea party Fridays in the treehouse?"

Sasha is trying not to laugh. *Is this a for-real question, or is he teasing me like usual, she thinks to herself.*

They both laugh.

Then Sasha says, "We haven't had a tea party since we were seven."

Rich looks at her, "Well, what do ya'll do up there on Fridays?"

"Strip poker," she says with a straight face.

Just then a flurry or colored lights start flashing over by Big Willy's booth. The overhead speakers turn up even louder, and everyone on this floor looks over to the booth.

All right Countdown kids, I have a BIG MISTLTOE KTOE announcement coming up after No. 17. See if you can guess what it is. Something big is coming to San Antonio just down the road from all of my TOE people. Here is a new song NOBODY has heard yet. My good buddy from LA ... you know who he is ... He sent me this song to try out on ya'll first before it goes national. Here it is No. 17, "Basketball Jones," by Cheech and Chong.

Cecilia is quickly writing a note to pass through to Big Willy.

"A Concert?" it reads.

Big Willy puts on the intercom speaker for just those by the booth. He acts like he is gonna say something, then smiles and shuts off the mic.

"Big Willy, you're mean," Cecilia yells at the booth.

Big Willy nearly falls back in his chair laughing.

Rich smacks his hand on Sasha's shoulder, "Come on" he says to her. They head over to where Izaak and Dom are.

"Hey, I think I know what the announcement is," he says to the other three.

"What?" Izaak looks stunned.

Rich almost says, then yells over to Cecilia, "Cecilia, come here!" She runs over. Rich hears tons of good inside stuff from his connections at Mistletoe Mansion.

Rich huddles them all up and starts to speak, then stops. "Hey, where are Wu and Izzy?"

"Library," Sasha says quickly. "Come on, spill."

"Izaak, go get the bookworm twins" Rich says to Izaak and he dashes up the stairs to the fourth floor. The other four wait impatiently.

"So, Dom, did you see the cute girl back at the block with the feathers in her hair?" Sasha asks. Rich tries to hold back a blush.

Dom looks at her puzzled. He is clueless.

Izaak leads the other two girls down the stairs. He is holding a book. Wu is complaining.

"I was in the middle of chapter five, you big moose" she yells at Izaak, trying to catch up.

They join the huddle.

Rich puts his arms around Sasha on his left and Dom on his right. He nods to the others to huddle up with their arms.

"Don't touch me, Moose." Wu is still put off.

The song above on the speakers is winding down.

"I have it on good authority that San Antonio is getting an ABA team from Dallas," Rich says and then looks over to the booth. "Basketball Jones" has ended.

You heard it here first, Countdown Kids. Let me know what you thought of that one. Call in or come on down and share some knowledge with Big Willy. Caller number 8 gets Puffy Tacos from the Gomez booth at Founders Day later this afternoon.

"That's where Zoltar is!" Dom says, poking Rich in the chest.

Here's the big news, San Antonio is getting an ABA team. The Dallas Chapparells are moving to SA. I hear they will be asking for a new name soon.

Keep it here for more details; now here is No. 16, brand new from Chicago, this is "Feeling Stronger Every Day."

"That's it!" Wu punches Izaak. "That's why you drug us down here?" She takes her book back.

"Uncool, man," Izzy chimes in, and the two girls head back up to the library.

Rich calls back to the girls, "We gonna still meet up for snacks at 9:30 on the front porch?"

Izzy turns back around and sticks out her tongue at Rich.

Dom and Izaak decide to go to the third floor where all the UTA sports cards are laid out in boxes. They want to see if any of last year's ABA Dallas cards are still available.

Rich calls back to Dom as he walks away, "You really think Zoltar is with his folks at the Puffy Taco booth?"

"Makes sense to me," Dom calls back.

Cecilia stays with Sasha and Rich looking at albums. But she quickly bores of it and pulls Sasha over to the singles section.

"Albums are better," Rich says smugly as he knows where Cecilia is going.

"Shut up, Richard," she huffs.

Rich smiles. *It is a good day,* he thinks to himself. But where is *Zoltar?* He has so much to tell him! New neighbors and new changes to the block.

Rich continues to look through the stacks of vinyl. He eventually settles on the Elton John album, a used copy of Who's Next that appears a little scratchy and a near vintage Yardbirds album. The last one is a pricey import, but Rich feels confident that it's worth it.

Snack time approaches, and the seven gather near the first-floor entrance to load up on snacks for the Founders Day parade. The booths can get expensive and don't always have the great selection that Pinky's has. Everybody gets a little sweet-tooth taste of something. Izzy is last to check out, and she is short thirteen cents.

"Dang it all to Hades and back," she exclaims, showing off a bit of her latest vocabulary from her library visit.

The lady clerk is not impressed.

A young adult, under thirty or so, is behind the gang and flicks a quarter to Izzy. "No problem, Miss, I've got you covered."

Izzy catches the quarter perfectly in her hand and gives it to the clerk. She looks at the coin in amazement. Izzy is probably the least ball-sports, hand-to-eye person in the group, yet she caught that perfectly. The others look at her with a similar stunned look. She even had to turn while the coin was in the air. *Zoltar would have caught that, no problem,* she thinks to herself. She looks up at the man.

"Thank you," she says.

All seven ten-year-olds stare at the man.

He smiles back at them and collects his coins from the clerk.

None of the seven say a word. They head out the front door past Chief Charlie's rocking chair. They pause and look back. The man is chatting up the store clerk. They seem to be flirting with each other.

The man stops in mid-sentence and quickly turns to the kids.

They scurry out of sight.

They run to their bikes, all stacked up twenty feet away from the main doors. They huddle up, sitting on and off the porch, going through their purchases. Dom looks through his new open pack of basketball cards. "Rich Jones," he says excitedly.

The others look at him.

"He was a Chaparral last year in Dallas," he says happily with new knowledge. "He's gonna be with San Antonio now!"

Cecilia looks at Dom's stacks of cards, "No baseball today?" she asks.

"Nah, I always get baseball cards with Zoltar ..." he trails off.

"Yeah, where the hell is Zoltar! He was with us last night," Rich says emphatically.

"Hell?" Wu questions. "Not even a H E double hockey sticks?"

"Yeah, *hell!*" Rich shoots back at her. "It's Founders Day—we all should be together for Founders Day."

"He's probably at the taco booth with his family," Dom says calmly.

"Dipstick!" Sasha says.

"What?" Dom says to Sasha.

"Zoltar, he's a dipstick for not being here," Sasha replies.

"Dipstick? Is that supposed to be a cuss word?" Wu asks, sipping on her Dr. Pepper. "Cuz if it is, it's pretty stupid."

Sasha glares at her.

"Asshole," Rich says defiantly.

"That's more like it! That gets a bar of soap out at my house for Mr. Potty Mouth." Wu smiles.

"Pendejo" Sasha says, and everybody reacts, "Ooooh!

"What does that mean?" Izaak asks.

"I don't know. Zoltar said that to a pitcher last week that struck him out, and the umpire ejected him," Sasha says with big eyes.

A quiet pause ensues while they all take a sip of their drinks.

"Booger," Dom breaks the silence, and they all laugh.

"Son of a biscuit!" Izaak adds a new one. "Dad says that when he is frustrated in the shop."

They each look around for any more forbidden words, and then all eyes settle on Izzy.

Izzy senses the vibe. All the eyes are upon her. She waits for the tension to build just enough, then she takes her lips off her straw. She sits up and says, "Caca," then burps very loud.

Everybody hoots and hollers and rolls around, happy to be happy.

Chief Charlie, the Lakota Tribal leader for Mistletoe, comes out and sits in his rocking chair next to where the group has parked their bikes. He smiles at the laughter. The man who was in line behind Izzy comes over and chats with Chief for a bit. He shakes his hand and starts to walk off, pausing to look at the kids. They stop and acknowledge his look. He nods in their direction and waves. He walks down the other end. As soon as he is out of sight, the kids all gather around Charlie.

"Who was that!" Sasha leads the questioning.

Chief Charlie settles in and pulls out his tobacco and a rolling paper. He takes his time. The kids give respect and wait for him patiently. He rolls his cigarette and reaches into three different pockets before finding his Zippo lighter. He lights it and takes a big drag. He flicks something off of his shirt and then is ready to answer the question. He settles back into his chair and begins rocking. He holds up his lit cigarette with his right hand.

"Mr. Lazarus," he says quietly. "He is the new fifth grade teacher at the school."

The kids remain quiet but take in the new information.

"Isn't it time for church?" Charlie asks out loud.

"Caca!" Sasha yells out loud, We gotta go!

"Thanks, Chief Charlie, we will all be back tonight for Founders Day story time!" Rich says and puts out his hand to shake.

Chief Charlie brings down his right hand, takes the cigarette with his left, cracks a wry smile, and shakes Rich's hand firmly.

They all hop on bikes. Cecilia puts her transistor into the basket and turns up the volume as loud as it can go for the ride back.

That was No. 3 on the countdown. "Shaved Fish" by the impromptu jam recorded at Eric Clapton's wedding to George Harrison's ex. John Lennon, Keith Richards, Eric Clapton, and Keith Moon! Wow, my invitation must still be in the mail. They call themselves the Dirty Mac. Just a single this time. Love to hear these guys together in a studio! Two more songs left after this commercial break ...

3

LUTHERAN ALPHABET JELLO

Rich and Dom get back to the treehouse alone. The others have dispersed to their houses and off to various churches of choice and tradition. Dom is ready to park his bike in his own yard when Rich stops him.

"Hey, what was the number one song this week, same as last?"

"Oh yeah," Dom smiles. "'Little Willy by the Sweet,' like twenty weeks in a row now."

"That Big Willy sure loves his Little Willy!" Rich says with a *big* smirk on his face.

They both laugh.

"That just sounds wrong!" Dom starts to walk his bike home.

"Hey, Dom, come here," Rich motions to his buddy.

Sensing something special, Dom stops and drops his bike by the basketball goal and comes over to the base of the tree by Rich.

"What's up?" he says with a whisper.

"Hey, uh, can you miss church this week?" Rich asks.

Dom thinks for a second but senses a buddy moment about to happen.

"Well, I kinda wanted to talk to Pastor after church about this dream I keep having. It's got to do with cornfields, skyscrapers, Jesus or church, or sumthin'," Dom says scratching his head.

"I wanna check out these new neighbors" Rich says almost pleading.

"Like spying, from the crow's nest?" Dom says excitedly.

Rich knows how much Dom likes to climb trees all over Mistletoe, and they do have the best treehouse crow's nest in the whole town.

"Yeah," Rich says, knowing he has his buddy convinced.

Dom leaves his bike and starts to climb. Rich follows. They get to the main level and grab the binoculars. Mr. Black absconded with them from way back while cleaning out Mistletoe Mansion stuff that looks like it was from the '50s. They climb up through the main level. Tulpen is still sleeping on her pillow. They keep climbing up to the crows' nest, which has just enough room for two people. They sit on sturdy wooden boxes, crafted by Mr. Black. The original idea for the nest was to be the main lookout during the annual water balloon fights that happen the last day of school every year. You can see over the houses to Woodlawn Lake past the Mansion and survey the entire school playgrounds behind them. To the left, they can see two blocks over into Sasha's backyard and into Magnolia street. Out the front—and where Rich wants to spy—the entire short Mistletoe Street block is laid out like a TV screen. Dom gets settled, and Rich doesn't even squawk when Dom gets the binoculars first.

"The girl in the skirt," he says while looking out.

"What, you see her?" Rich says way too happily.

Dom looks at his buddy and realizes why he is really here. "No, I just figured you were sweet on her from earlier," Dom says with a smile.

Blushing, Rich smiles back and just says, "Yeah, I kinda liked what I saw, she's ..." He pauses to get the right word. "Mysterious."

The two boys sit patiently and watch mostly the MDS guys finish unloading boxes for the two families. The two dads are struggling with a big barbeque smoker on a cart. They are trying to wheel it into the backyard of No. 2104. They open the side fence gate, and the dogs get loose again. They get the barbeque into the back, but the MDS workers have to help coral the dogs again. It is mildly entertaining.

After about a half hour of nothing else special happening, they hear a meow from below. They look down and see Tulpen fussing at them from the ladder hole below. Dom looks down at her and tries to convey a sense of "keep quiet." She blinks at him with both eyes. Just then we see a young boy about Dom and Rich's age coming from the left. No. 2105 is next to Dom's house. The boys try hard to get quieter.

Chad Simms is walking toward the basketball goal with a black, yellow, red, and white ABA ball under his arms. He is not dribbling. This seems odd because what boy with a ball ready to shoot hoops doesn't dribble? Dom and Rich look at each other sensing the weirdness at the same time. Rich takes the binoculars. He looks over to the mysterious girl's house but sees nothing. He looks back to the boy with the ball. There is noise. A smaller boy runs up behind the boy with the ball and pokes it out of his arms. The boy doesn't even flinch, like he knew it was coming.

Dom swivels his head quietly toward Rich and whispers one word, "Brothers," he says and Rich nods his head.

The younger boy dribbles up to the goal and puts in a perfect layup. The older boy catches up and gets directly under the goal. The younger boy lines up some outside shots and makes most of them, with the older boy rebounding and passing the ball back out to his brother. This goes on for about fifteen minutes when Dom nudges Rich with his elbow. Rich is still with the binoculars trying to figure out which window at No. 2104 could be the mysterious girl's room. Dom whispers to Rich, "Deacon." Rich looks down to the basketball goal and sees Dom's twin brother walking out from No. 2107. Deacon walks up to the boys shooting and stands on the edge of the court. The younger one sees him and without hesitation passes him the ball. "Wanna play?" he calls out.

Deacon gets the ball, dribbles a bit, and launches a ten footer. Swish. Deacon then looks right up to the crow's nest and makes eye contact with Dom and Rich. They both crouch down at having been discovered. Deacon sees them but doesn't say a word.

"Hi, I'm Jordan and this is my brother Chad," the younger one says. He dribbles and shoots a layup. "We are named after foreign countries. We have two younger sisters named Kiribati and Fiji." He passes the ball to Deacon. He catches it and does the classic guy head nod to Chad. Chad nods back. They have now officially met.

"My name is Deacon," he says and shoots the ball.

Rich and Dom are still crouched down, not wanting to be seen. They listen to the dribbling and shooting sounds for a moment until they feel it's safe to watch again.

Jordan keeps chattering, "We just moved here to Mistletoe from Native Lands in the Black Hills. You ever been there?"

Deacon shakes his head no and takes another shot.

"We moved here with the Stones. Our mothers are best friends from Lakota." Jordan can't stop chattering. "Our dads love to barbeque, and we are gonna have a big party tonight at 8 after all the Founders Day stuff. We were gonna have it earlier but just heard about all the food at the lake. My sisters are making flyers and putting them on everybody's door."

Chad just smiles and keeps rebounding.

"You like ABA teams or NBA teams?" Jordan asks. "I hear San Antonio is gonna get the Chaparrals, can you believe that?"

"I like the NBA I guess. The O'Cherokees are pretty good," Deacon says.

"They just won the championship!" Jordan says.

Chad nods approval and sends a rebound back out to Jordan.

"O'Cherokees are pathetic!" a new voice enters. A big boy wearing an O'Cherokees junior NBA jersey number 33 walks up with the mystery girl right behind him.

"Luke Stone," he says and extends a hand to Deacon. Luke has a long black ponytail and looks to be pure native tribe. He is slightly bigger than Deacon, like maybe he's twelve years old. "That's my kid sister Stacy"

"Stacy," Rich says all dreamy like. Rich is now fidgety.

The mystery girl in her black-and-white plaid skirt and black tank top walks around the edge of the court and to the bench just behind the goal. She makes eye contact with Chad and sits down to survey the situation. She crosses her legs lady like, and Rich notices her sweet black Chuck Taylor high tops. The only color about her is the long lilac purple feathers flowing from her hair in three different spots. She looks like a ten-year-old, like them, but much more sophisticated.

"I like Johnny Brown Horse from the O'Cherokees," Deacon says after shooting from the top of the key. He looks at Luke for a response.

Tapping the No. 33 on his jersey, Luke says, "Brown Horse is the best player in the NBA." He smiles and then gets the ball from Chad. He dribbles in place and between his legs, posturing a bit. He spins the native-colored ABA ball in his hands, "I guess I just prefer the ABA," He shoots and swishes and smiles at Deacon.

"Cool," Deacon says back. A lifelong-bonded friendship has just begun.

The boys team up for some two on two. Chad and Jordan match up against Deacon and Luke. Jordan runs around a lot and makes a ton of shots. Chad lets him do all the work. Chad sets screens and passes and rebounds. Jordan shoots everything. They have obviously done this before. Deacon and Luke pair up nicely and play well off each other for the first time. They keep it close but eventually lose 11–8 to the brothers.

Stacy Stone sits quietly the whole time. She is content to be watching. She seems to know Chad very well but can't take her eyes off of Deacon. When the game is over and the boys go over for a drink of water from the hose in Deacon's yard, Stacy gets up and shoots the ball. She dribbles and hits a few outside shots, but she keeps looking at whatever Deacon is doing.

Rich sees all of this and is getting jealous in his own calm and quiet way. Dom knows better than to say a word.

The boys wander back from getting water, and Stacy is still holding onto the ball. They are ready for a second game. Deacon comes up to her with his hand out, wanting the ball, "Do you play?" he asks. She looks at him funny when he speaks.

"You don't sound like you," she says to him clutching the ball.

Just then Tulpen meows loudly, getting everyone's attention. She has quietly come down from the treehouse and is now on the bench behind the goal where Stacy was sitting. Stacy turns and gets very happy. She drops the ball and yells, "Oh my God!" and goes quickly over to Tulpen. She picks up the cat and cradles her in her arms. This seems odd, but it is obvious that Stacy is very gentle and close to cats. She walks back over to Deacon and looks him straight in the eyes while he stands ready for another chance at shooting. Tulpen is purring in her arms as if they have been friends for life.

Stacy collects her thoughts and then says very defiantly, "You're not the one." She pauses a bit, petting Tulpen happily. "You look like him, but you are not the same boy from my dream." She is still staring into Deacon's eyes, but he does not flinch or seem weirded out by this.

Still looking back into Stacy's eyes, he dribbles a few bounces between his legs like he saw Luke do and then collects the ball onto his hip and says, " I am a twin."

Dom gasps and grabs Rich's arm, "That's where I have seen her before!" he holler-whispers at Rich! She's the girl from my dream!"

Pleasant Valley Lutheran (PVL) sits on the North side of Fred Road just outside the Mistletoe walls in what is technically San Antonio. Mistletoe doesn't actually have any churches inside the town walls but instead encouraged churches to spring up on Fred road. This section is commonly called Church Row. PVL is the Lutheran Church of America church in Lutheran world. The Lutheran Church Missouri Synod church, Redeemer, sits catty cornered from it on the south side of the street across from the Piggly Wiggly grocery store.

Pleasant Valley is the church that Dom and Rich are members of but are skipping this morning. Izzy Davinci is a member there with her family. Wu and Cecilia have decided to visit with her today. They like to attend each other's churches to learn and see which one they like best. Vacation Bible School season has already begun, and the girls like checking out all the different programs, as they are very social.

Cecilia is a member at the Baptist church. Her and her mom were there together until she died. Cecilia keeps her membership there as a tribute. Mr. Black and Izaak attend the Muslim mosque now. Wu likes to claim her possible Hindu roots with her adopted family, but she refuses to join any church as a member. Instead she enjoys learning from all faiths and visits each of the friends' churches. She calls it church shopping.

The three have come into Pleasant Valley a bit late, so they ascend to the balcony. There are a few high schoolers in the very back. Wu climbs into a pew in the front row, then Izzy sits in the middle, and Cecilia sits on Izzy's right side. She has her spiral notebook out with her scribbled version of Big Willy's top 40.

"So tell me again what the LCA means again?" Wu asks Izzy.

"Lutheran Church in America," Izzy says for like the fifth time this summer.

"So it's not ALC, like Zion over on Cincinnati street right?" Wu asks quizzically.

"I can't believe Big Willy keeps playing Little Willy as the No. 1. That joke is getting so old!" Cecilia says to no one in particular. They stand for the hymn.

"Zion is an American Lutheran Church" she says then adds before Wu can ask, "ALC is more of a German background, and LCA is more Scandinavian."

"Right, right …" Wu is remembering.

"All four Beatles in the top 5 … I wish they would get back together," Cecilia says while paging through the hymn looking for No. 654.

"Come together," Izzy says very plainly

"What?" Cecilia says at the interrupted thought.

"Come together," Izzy says with a straight face. "The proper English is Come together, not get back," she says with a teacher's voice.

Cecilia stares back at her dumbfounded.

"It's a whole 'nother song," Izzy says with a bit of a twang.

Cecilia smacks her with the hymnal.

"Sasha is a member at Redeemer LCMS across the street" Wu says confidently

"Right," Izzy says.

Wu leans over in deep thought, "LCMS is a whole different thing," she says with half authority and half questioning. "Lutheran Church Missouri Synod?"

"Right, no lady pastors in LCMS. We have a lady pastor," Izzy teaches.

"And that's a new thing?" Wu hunts for confirmation.

"Right," Izzy says, following the song but not singing.

On cue, the lady pastor steps up to the lectern to read the lessons. Elvira Barbara Blatzerelli is the fifth lady LCA pastor in Texas and the first in the San Antonio/Mistletoe area. She goes by Pastor EB. Izzy likes her because she has some Scandinavian Italian in her background, just like Izzy and her triplet sisters. Pastor EB can always tell Izzy apart from her other triplets because she never sits together with them. Pastor EB looks up to the balcony to make eye contact with Izzy. Izzy takes sermon notes on a bulletin so she can ask a deep question to try and trip up the pastor.

Cecilia pages through her spiral and then leans over to Izzy, "You ever heard of this Christian rocker Big Willy played today? Larry Norman?"

Izzy keeps eyes front and just shakes her head no.

"Sounds pretty cool, kinda racy lyrics for a Christian," Cecilia says to her notebook.

"Is she the only pastor?" Wu whispers on Izzy's other side.

Izzy nods yes.

"Please rise for the Gospel from the fifth chapter of Mark, verses 21–43 …" Pastor EB reads.

Izzy looks over to Cecilia's top 40 notes and asks, "What's your top five songs from the countdown" she does this knowing Cecilia will pour over her list and make her own selections. She will collect at least ten songs and whittle them down to the five asked for. She does this so Cecilia will be quiet for at least fifteen minutes on this task.

Izzy picks a Bible out of the rack in front of her. She hands it to Wu and asks, "I wonder how many times women are mentioned in the book of Mark." Wu's eyebrows raise up, and she takes the book and quickly turns to the passages in the Gospel.

Izzy sits up straight ahead and smiles. *Twenty minutes easily,* she thinks to herself.

Pastor EB finishes the Gospel lesson and begins her sermon:

"The Woman's Faith Set Her Free!"

The three young ladies climb down from the balcony after the service and get in line to shake Pastor's hands by the door. Cecilia has been working in her notebook and has written on the bulletin her top 5 from the day. She hands it to Izyy.

"Thanks!" She smiles at Cecilia who is still clueless as to why she really asked for the list. It reads as follows:

That Larry Norman song: (Gotta ask Pinky for the album)

"Shaved Fish" (love that Keith Richards)

"Wildflower" by Skylark

"One of a Kind Love Affair" by Spinners: makes me dance!

Barry White—anything by Barry is the best!

Izzy looks over to Wu and asks what number she came up with.

"I didn't count, I just read the whole book," she looks at Izzy with a sarcastic face.

"You could've just asked me to be quiet."

Izzy reaches out with a hand and a smile to her best friend. Wu takes her hand and smiles back.

"What question do you have for the pastor?" Wu asks. Izzy hands her the bulletin.

Wu looks at the bulletin and gives a positive nod back to Izzy. They get to the door where Pastor EB is shaking hands. Izzy hands her the bulletin and says, "Do you know my friend Cecilia?"

"Nice to meet you, Miss Cecilia," Pastor says and glances down at the bulletin. "See you ladies for VBS in two weeks?"

"Yes, maam!" Izzy says joyfully.

The three girls catch up with the Davinci family and head for the elevated train stop. They all hop on and head back around the edge of Mistletoe and the scenic route to home.

"See you at the fairgrounds?" Cecilia asks the other two ladies.

"I'll be late; save me a spot. I have a yard to mow," Izzy says.

"Sasha will meet us all at the Gomez booth" Cecilia says confidently.

"Bossha Sasha," Wu says, and they all laugh.

4

IT'S NOT A CUL-DE-SAC

The Black family walks to the Lake Street Station and climbs the platform to wait for the short ride to the parking garage just outside the Mistletoe walls where they have a perfect view of the parade route. While on the platform waiting for the train, Rich is still concerned about Zoltar's whereabouts. He scans the park grounds south, around Woodlawn Lake, where the food booths and snow cone carts and barbeque barrels have been set up, cooking since last night. Zoltar has never helped with prep before for the Gomez family booth, but this could be a first. He uses the binoculars and finds the Gomez booth just as the train comes in, but no Zoltar.

"Hey, Izaak, there aren't any extra baseball games you know of that Zoltar would be going to this weekend, do you?" he asks with a slight pitiful tone.

"Nope," Izaak responds. "It's July; baseball is over."

Izaak and Mr. Black are looking east of the lake and into the backyard of a house that has a small treehouse-like structure in it.

"I think that one's new this summer 'Zaak. I spotted it on Thursday," he says to his son.

Izaak reaches for the binoculars from Rich.

"I see it," Izaak says excitedly.

"How many in town is that now?" Cecilia asks.

"Seven by last count, and we put up the first one," Mr. Black exclaims proudly. They all four enter the train.

Rich brings up the rear. There is only standing room for him as the other three grab a seat bench. Before the doors close, there is a rushed commotion of noise.

"Hold the door!" someone yells. A man behind Rich holds open the door, and a whole crowd of people, seemingly together, hop on. Rich spins around to look and is face-to-face with Chad Simms. Chad smiles at him. His teeth are big and white under his sunglasses.

Mr. Black hops up and extends a hand to Chad's dad. "Hello, Mr. Simms."

Mr. Simms extends a hand back while making sure his crew got on the train, "I think we got them all. Please call me Chile!"

"Like winter or the country?" Mr. Black asks.

"Ha ha, very good. You catch on quick—like the country actually," he says in a slightly recognizable British accent.

"I must admit, I already knew," Mr. Black says, "I am caretaker for the block, and I got your info and the Stone family info before ya'll arrived," Mr. Black says. "I am glad ya'll made it for Founders Day. We had ya'll coming in next week"

"Change of plans, our Miss Stacy advised we get in early, lots to see with the parades and the scent of all the great food!" Chile says matter-of-fact like and looks over to Stacy seated by the door. Rich has not taken his eyes off of her. He keeps peeking around Chad to get a glimpse.

"Glad you made it. All settled in so far?" Mr. Black inquires.

"Oh certainly, boxes and boxes! Mr. Black, you have me at a disadvantage. What is your first name, sir?"

"Yes, yes, I am Odafin Black, but you can call me Fin." He smiles and continues, "This is my son Izaak, my daughter Cecilia, and our adopted son, Richard Mistletoe the fourth."

"Very good, very good," Chile settles in with a handrail and sways to the ride.

"Chile, are ya'll headed to the parade?" Fin asks.

"Yes," he says and counts all the heads of the two families, making sure they made it on board. "Looks like all ten made it!"

As the dads talk and talk, Rich decides to introduce himself to Stacy. He transfers hand holds over to the spot in front of the door next to

Stacy. She is looking outside through the big window. Just as he opens his mouth to speak, the train pulls into the station.

Stacy hops up and calls out, "Chad!" As she brushes past Rich to connect with Chad, she smiles briefly at Rich. He follows her and pivots around to see Stacy take Chad's hand, and they exit with the others.

Rich, the Blacks, the Simms, and the Stone families all join together to watch the parade from the best vantage point possible. The train lets them off near the registration depot just outside Big Gate No. 3 that all new Mistletoe residents come through. Everybody else who enters Mistletoe to live does so at the hospital on the east end of town. These parade watchers are just outside the Mistletoe wall in San Antonio at the parking garage on the fourth floor. This spot is choice because you can look onto the corner of St. Cloud and Woodlawn inside the Mistletoe gates where the parade turns.

At this turn, the people on foot or horseback head up the ramp to the grand walkway that goes through the heart of Mistletoe. The rest of the parade vehicles continue under the train platform. The Grand Woodlawn Avenue walkway is above the train and only a single row of chairs are lined up to watch the various dancers and performers and walkers that process past the lake and the main pathway. The most anticipated group to pass by are the Teddy Roosevelt "Ruff Riders." They are a group of tye-dye hippies from the organic grocery store who dress up their dogs like Founder Teddy Roosevelt and march along while other hippie employees play songs from the '60s on recorders.

Rich angles and maneuvers his way to get close to Stacy and Chad as they sit on dropped tailgates of the family trucks in the garage to watch. He is building up the nerve when he looks down to the street to where Sasha and Wu's family have set up near the Grand Hotel entrance. It is also on the corner. Sasha is waving feverishly at Rich and shouting something he can't hear. He is distracted, trying to understand her yelling over the marching bands that are passing by in between them. Izaak and Cecilia pass in front of him and directly over to Chad and Stacy.

"Hello," Cecilia says to Stacy. "My name is Cecilia."

What is she doing? Rich fumes to himself. Every time he gets up the nerve to talk to Stacy, something happens.

"And this is Rich," Cecilia says to Stacy and Chad, gesturing over to Rich.

Rich smiles.

He freezes up and looks back across the street at Sasha jumping up and down, arms waving like a crazy lady. He also notices other eyes on him. One section over is Mr. Lazarus from the store earlier. He is by himself but looking up right at Stacy and Chad.

"Oh hey, there's Sasha and Wu; they are friends of ours also," Cecilia says and now Chad, Stacy, Izaak, and Cecilia are all waving at Sasha and Wu.

Rich sits on the tailgate and stews, missing a great chance to visit with his friends and make new friends. Izaak occasionally looks over to him and gives him the what's-up look. *How does Izaak know I like her,* Rich wonders to himself. *Maybe Dom told him? Maybe Sasha said something—nah, when did Sasha meet Stacy.* All these thoughts running through his head.

The parade is over, and the whole viewing crew decides to walk around the big Taste of Mistletoe fairgrounds at Woodlawn Lake. This is the best part of Founders Day. The entire cultural experience of Mistletoe is on display. The dancers are on side stages. There are skits and plays and poetry readings, as well as pow wow rituals. The main stage has all the KTOE DJs, and there is talk of a major band closing the show. Right now, Cecilia is headed over with a buffalo burger on a stick to hear a local Mistletoe band called Skunk Fart. Sasha and Wu meet up with the group, and they dive into the smells and sounds of the biggest party of the year. Rich walks along dejected.

"Hey, Rich," Stacy pulls away from the group and walks up to Rich.

He starts to freeze, but then a wave of calm comes over him. He can't explain it to his brain, but he suddenly feels at home in her presence.

"You feeling OK?" she says and puts a hand on his shoulder.

"Yeah, just been missing my buddy Zoltar, I haven't seen him since our sleepover in the treehouse last night. I am worried about him," he says as intelligent and poignant words tumble out of his mouth while his heart doubles its beat.

Stacy stops. Her hand on his shoulder holds him from walking forward. She pauses and closes her eyes. She appears to be in a thinking trance. Her left hand is twitching a bit by her side. The right hand on his shoulder is warm and very reassuring.

She opens her eyes and looks deep into his. "I am not sure where he is, but I get a sense that he is happy and doing well," she says into Rich's soul very gently.

Rich takes it in. Her eyes are a brilliant violet color. He looks deep into them, memorizing the colors and wondering where he might find other examples of this color in nature.

She smiles back at him with a bit of a wisdom, as if she has seen this expression before when someone looks deep into her eyes.

"Yeah," Rich says and takes his hands out of his pockets. Not feeling dejected anymore, he just says "Yeah" again. He puts his left hand on hers that still has his shoulder immobilized.

"Come on, let's get some food. Hey, are you gonna join our big family barbeque back on the block tonight?" she says taking his hand and leading him back into the group.

"Yeah," he says in a very happy mood.

They start to catch up and head toward all the food booths.

"Oh, hey, I meant to ask you, have you seen Dom? He has a twin brother Deacon, that I met earlier playing basketball," she asks.

"No, he has a family thing downtown with his aunt or something," he says and realizes she is holding his hand. He also realizes that he doesn't feel jealous of Dom for holding Stacy's attention without even being here. Girls always ask where Dom is.

It is a very festive afternoon. Everyone in the group is enjoying new friendships with Chad and Stacy. Only Dom and Izzy and Zoltar are missing. They stop by the Gomez family tamale hut, but only cousins and other family are there. Rich doesn't speak any Spanish, and he is not as worried about his buddy now that Stacy has calmed his nerves. The Stones and the Simms are fun families. The moms are quiet with everybody but each other. The dads are goofy, and the little sisters pass out way too many flyers. By 2 o'clock, the dads decide to go back to the house and tend to the brisket on the big smokers. Cecilia is beside herself. She finds out Foghat will be the closing band at 10 tonight before the fireworks. Skunk Fart was pretty good, she reports, for a high school band.

The only downside to the day has been the debate over the hand-designed flyers that the two new Simms girls have been handing out and promoting. It says clearly to meet at the "2100 cul-de-sac on Mistletoe Street." Every adult and youth on the block noticed this mistake and has nicely tried to correct it.

"It's not a cul-de-sac!" Sasha said a bit loudly to Mr. Stone when handed a flyer by the girls.

"Oops, we'll get that fixed" he replied, but the girls have made fifty handmade copies, and no one really had the heart to make them do them over. All is more than forgiven when the block families and friends come back home around supper time to get some of the barbeque that the new dads have been cooking all day.

Around sunset, before too much light leaves the block on this long summer day, a kickball game breaks out. Jordan Simms gets it going with his boundless energy. He brings out a big red playground bouncy ball and declares a parents-versus-kids kickball game. The dads are game and start recruiting all able-bodied adults to join. Grandma Maxwell just cackles with glee when she is invited to join but declines. Mr. Black is very game and convinces Sasha's mom to play first base. She gets her two adult sons to come out as ringers. Sasha's dad comes out too. The baseball game on his TV is over. Eight adults total were recruited.

Jordan gets Luke to set up home base in the middle of the cobblestone and grass street just in front of both new households. First base is the big palm tree in Dom's yard near the sidewalk. Second base is the picnic table by the basketball hoop. The kids bring it out from behind the hoop where it lives and up to the right distance for a kickball diamond. Third base is the stump in the Hamilton's front yard at No. 2106. The teams get assembled, and Jordan holds court as the pitcher. There are twelve or more kids at any time when not finishing ice cream or watermelon. He declares that the game will be won automatically if anyone can kick the ball into the basketball hoop directly from "centerfield."

The game goes well, and the block is taking on a new sense of fun and togetherness that only the kids on the block seemed to have the last few years. They need a better name. The very shy thirteen-year-old Steve Hamilton even comes out to play a few innings. His grandma sits on the porch, lighting up a big cigar and cheering her grandson on when he kicks one into "left field" over the Mistletoe Mansion wall next to the Hamilton house. Grandma Maxwell sees an opportunity and brings a food plate over with Mrs. Simms and Mrs. Stone. Mr. Fremont makes an appearance on his upper deck at No. 2103. He waves while holding up his fifth beer.

Stacy claims to be playing second base but does so by sitting on the picnic bench and talking to each runner who comes to her choice spot. Rich is tagged out at second base in like the fourth inning, and Stacy asks him to sit with her. He does, panting from running his fastest.

"Hey, nice try," she says, putting a hand on his right shoulder "I thought you were safe."

"Thanks," he says with no lack of shyness or embarrassment. There is something about Stacy's touch and being that seems to calm everybody near her. Rich can't explain it to himself, but he certainly feels it.

"Dom isn't coming back tonight is he?" she asks getting straight to a point.

"No, the Blues have family in downtown San Antonio, and I think they stay the night sometimes," Rich says taking a bandana out of his back pocket and wiping his face.

"I need a favor," she says and makes subtle yet intense eye contact with Rich.

"Anything," he says without hesitation.

"I need to borrow one of Dom's shirts," she says.

"Um, OK," he says with curious eyes.

"Here's the thing, I have these dreams every night, and they tell me things," she says

"OK" Rich responds.

"I convinced our families to move here a week early because of dreams I had all last month. I kept seeing Dom in this dream. I thought it was Deacon at first, but I know now it was Dom," she says with Rich giving her his full attention.

"If I can wear someone's clothing when I sleep, the dreams become clearer about that person."

She lets all this info sink in.

At that moment, Chad is up to kick and sends a perfect arc of the ball over Stacy and Rich's heads and directly into the basket. Swish. Game over.

Everybody is yelling and screaming. Chad runs around the bases like Roberto Clemente on a respectful home-run trot.

Rich never loses eye contact with Stacy. He thinks calmly, then speaks.

"We got our team Rhino basketball jerseys for our junior league up in the treehouse." He says with mass commotion going on all around him. "Tulpen is probably sleeping on them in the box"

"The cat?" Stacy asks, "Tulpen?"

"Yeah, come on up. Dom's No. 37 should be in there." Rich takes her hand, and they walk to the treehouse.

"Why is her name Tulpen?" she asks.

"It's the name on her collar," Rich says.

"Interesting," Stacy responds.

5

CHIEF CHARLEY

The final part of every Founders Day celebration for the Mistletoe kids on the block is to sit at the feet of Chief Charley and hear the story of the Lakota and their part in the history of the making of this great little town. The firepit on the porch of Pinky's Store is stoked and crackling. The usual eight are not all present. Dom and Zoltar are not here tonight. It is the first time both have missed in recent memory. In their place, Chad and Stacy have been invited to join Rich, Izzy, Cecilia, Izaak, Wu, and Sasha. The kids are dragging a bit, wiped out from the number of events and excitement from an outstanding day. It is time to chill with Chief Charley and relax at the end of the day, except for Cecilia who still has energy. Her mind is on Foghat and the concert conclusion at the park in less than an hour. The kids park their bikes in the same place as this morning.

Stacy rides on the back of Chad's bike because she has no bike. Rich notices and thinks to himself that their friend Toby Windwalker could find them a bike for Stacy. Toby lives next door to Zoltar—where is Zoltar?

At the feet of Chief Charley's rocker, the kids assemble. Charley is anxious to meet the two new kids and motions for Stacy to come closer.

"What is your full name, young lady?" Charley asks from a sitting up position. He is looking into her violet eyes.

"Stacy Long Feather Stone," she says after standing up and presenting herself respectfully.

"Mmm Hmmmm" Charley acknowledges. He motions for her to sit down.

He turns his attention to Chad, "And you, sir, full name please."

Chad stands and takes the same stance as Stacy before him.

"Chad Grey Fox Simms," he says confidently and with a low voice. The others realize these are the first words they have heard Chad speak the whole day they have spent around him and Stacy. Charley leans back and motions him to sit back down as well. He settles back into his rocker and rocks gently for a minute, pondering. The fire is the only noise they hear.

He then sits up to address his patient, small tribe of attentive story time listeners.

"I won't be retelling the tale this evening" he says calmly. There are a few groans of disappointment.

He looks to Rich. "You, sir, will tell the tale at a later time when it is right to do so." He pauses for effect. "There is a pressing issue that you, my young warriors need to prepare for."

The kids look at each other curiously. Rich begins to say something, and Charley senses it.

"You are ready," He says directly to Richard Mistletoe IV.

Charley leans forward, and the kids follow his lead.

"There are ten of you now and more coming. Your small tribe has important tasks ahead." He has their full attention.

"I don't have all the answers, but there is a reason that Long Feather and Grey Fox have joined us from the Tribal Lands. They bring purpose and near completion to a great task and adventure ahead." He sits back and rocks while choosing his words carefully.

Sasha speaks up, "What adventure, Chief Charley?"

He starts to reach for his tobacco and lighter, then stops and sits up again with regained strength. Chief Charley is close to 100 years old, so say the elders.

"I have had newfound visions for a long month, two words keep coming to my lips and my dreams," he says and tries to sit up again. Rich and Izaak stand and gently cradle each of Charley's arms so he can sit up tall in his chair.

"One word comes from your past," he is looking at Grey Wolf. "You are descended from the Jewish tribes?" Chad nods yes.

"The word is Saducee. Do you know what it means?" Chad shakes his head no.

Izaak and Rich can feel strength leaving his body, and they are practically holding him up.

"The other word is Tulpen. She is your cat?" He looks at Stacy.

Stacy does not know how to respond.

Sasha speaks up, "Tulpen is all of ours, I guess. She lives in the treehouse or with Dominix in his room. She climbs the branches from the treehouse and crosses from tree to tree until she gets to Dom's bedroom window. He keeps it open for her all year."

Chief nods and smiles, "How long has she been with you?" he asks.

The kids look at each other. No one can remember when she came to the block.

Rich speaks up, "She has been around as long as we can remember." The others nod yes.

Chief sits back again with his full weight into the comfort of his nesting chair. He seems to be losing all of his strength. Izaak and Rich sit back down.

Chief pauses for a long time now, scratching his chin, then stroking the end of his ponytail that rests on his chest. He seems to be storing up energy, and then he sits up without any help and appears to be stronger, briefly.

"You must keep Tulpen safe from the Saducee," he says and looks into each of the kids eyes for validation of his request. He then sits back and begins to rock gently.

"How do we do that?" Sasha asks boldly.

"Your teacher will help you," Charley says without looking at any of them but instead stares into the fire.

Sasha starts to ask another question. Chief holds up his left hand from the arm of the chair, and she remains quiet.

"That is all I have for you, my children. Take care of each other, and inform the others," He says calmly. "Be on your way." Then he looks at Cecilia and says, "The music awaits."

They each get up and touch Charley's left hand as it is raised for a solemn goodbye. They head to their bikes and ride back quickly and quietly to the treehouse, dropping their bikes, as all gather and stare at each other, looking for leadership. They are awkwardly standing around the base of the tree, realizing they won't all fit in the treehouse where the boys have left their sleeping bags.

Stacy speaks up first, "Tulpen isn't there; she left for Dom's window when Rich and I were up there after the kickball game."

Rich nods.

Sasha speaks next, "I think we should have a meeting in the deck house and try and figure out what Chief Charley was saying. It seems really important." She looks at Cecilia who is usually antsy when she is late for something.

"I aint going anywhere," she says with a tone in her voice that is both excited and scared.

Stacy says calmly and with a questioning tone, "No?" She connects with the others' eyes. "Chief said the music awaits. I think you should go."

Sasha looks at Stacy with joined authority, "She's right, Izzy, you go with her and watch for anything different at the concert. Anything ... meaningful."

"From Foghat?" Cecilia ponders out loud.

"And take a walkie talkie with you," Sasha says

"What are ya'll gonna do?" Izzy asks.

"I think the rest of us should meet and figure out what to do about Tulpen and this Saducee thing," Sasha says with the voice of leadership and cool sensibility.

Stacy nods to her.

"Rich, you and Izaak make *totally* sure Tulpen is up in Dom's room, then meet us behind Hamilton's house," Sasha directs. "Anybody need to check in with parents or can we all stay up a little longer?"

"I'm good for the concert with Cecilia," Izzy says picking up her bike.

"My folks know I am staying at your house tonight," Wu says looking at Sasha.

"I'm good," Rich says.

"I'm hungry," Izaak says. Chad nods in agreement with Izaak.

"We can check in at home and then meet back there," Stacy says to Chad and points to the gravel path between the Hamilton house and the

Mistletoe Mansion's brick wall.

"Yup, just down the path next to the Blacks' place behind Hamiltons,'" Sasha affirms, impressed with Stacy's feel for the block and its layout.

Rich and Izaak take off between Sasha and Dom's house and start to climb the tree outside Dom's window.

The deck house is like a treehouse but is actually a deck built around a tree. It is supported by legs that connect it to the ground and keep it stable. It resides behind the Hamiltons' five-story house at No. 2106, just past their property line. The tree line and tall chain-link fence behind the deck house separate the Black family property and Woodlawn Avenue and the elevated train. On the other side of Woodlawn Avenue is the lake, the park, and in the south corner, the concert where Foghat is going on soon. The deck house is behind Mr. Black's overgrown garage shed.

The Black family, with Rich who isn't officially adopted by the Blacks, live in the upstairs part of the double-wide garage. It is one of the few garages left since no cars are allowed to drive in Mistletoe. The deck house is very sturdy and enclosed on the upper portion. A railed walkway attaches the second floor of the garage with the upper floor of the deck house. There is enough room for a dozen or so people on the main deck floor which sits only three feet off the ground, like a deck. Mr. Black built the whole thing before Izaak was old enough to help. Izaak bunks in the upper part with Rich most of the year until it gets too cold. Rich could live in the Mistletoe Mansion, but it creeps him out too much.

Cecilia has a room in the garage's upper part where there is a small kitchen and full bathroom. Mr. Black spends much of his time in the garage where all his tools and projects keep him busy. He has a couch and a TV and a big fridge to keep him happy. His light is usually always on, and he routinely forgets to close the garage doors when he falls asleep watching Johnny Carson. Mr. Black was given the property and the garage by the Mistletoe family as part of his job as caretaker of the Mistletoe Mansion and Tourist Museum. He has saved up enough money to buy an actual house in Mistletoe, but the kids love the block and treehouse and the community of people right here. It appears that, with the Stones and the Simms moving in so effortlessly, no one is moving.

Chad and Izaak are the last to join the group for the meeting. They are both eating sandwiches, and Chad is carrying a Tupperware container.

"Chad's mom made PB and Js!" Izaak says with a full mouth. "Strawberry!"

They climb up the stairs and into the covered outdoor space that has nice chairs scattered around a glass table. Sasha and Stacy are sitting and chatting. Wu has the receiving walkie talkie and is listening for a report from Cecilia and Izzy. Rich is pacing slowly along the back of the deck.

"Tulpen is fine; she's asleep on Dom's bed," Stacy says to Chad and Izaak.

"She's out like a light," Rich says and sits down around the table. Chad hands him a sandwich.

"Chad's mom is the coolest!" Izaak says with another mouthful.

All gathered, they are about to start the meeting, when a black cat hops up onto the railing, startling Wu who drops the walkie.

"Tabitha!" Stacy bursts out, "Come here, girl."

Wu picks up the walkie talkie, "Tabitha? What kind of name is that?"

"Bewitched," Rich says with his head on the table.

"Bewitched? What's that? Like a curse?" Wu asks.

Rich lifts his head up, "It's from the TV show" Tabitha jumps up onto the table and rubs against Rich's arms as they hold his tired head up. Tabitha walks over to sit in Stacy's lap.

They all sit around the table.

"Ya'll are tired. It's been a long day, so maybe we should just keep Tulpen guarded and worry about Chief Charley's warnings later," Sasha says to a few moans from Rich and Wu.

"I'm good, got energy now," Izaak says, holding up another sandwich. Chad smiles with a full mouth and jelly on his cheek.

The walkie talkie startles Wu and crackles.

"Green Rhino, come in. Foghat girl to Green Rhino!" Cecilia's voice comes through loud and clear. Fainter but, still audible we hear Izzy's voice in the background. "Green Rhino? You sound like the boys; give me that."

Stacy looks at Sasha while Izzy wrestles the walkie talkie from Wu. "What's a Green Rhino?" she whispers.

"It's our junior league basketball team. All the teams are Rhinos because of the high school, and each team is a different color." Stacy nods understanding. She is wearing Dom's Green Rhino jersey under her baggy t-shirt.

"Hey, Sasha," the walkie perks up again with Izzy's voice.

"Wu here, go ahead; we are all together."

"We are at the show, and you will never guess who is here?"

"Go ahead," Sasha says authoritatively

"Mr. Lazarus from this morning at the store," Izzy says.

The others look around at each other. Rich perks up from his fatigue.

"Didn't Chief Charley say he was a teacher?" Izzy asks.

Sasha reaches for the walkie from Wu, "Yes he did. What's he doing?"

There is a staticky noise, then Cecilia's voice comes on, "He stays close to where we are. I think he's watching us. We are gonna split up and see what happens."

"Where are you now?" Sasha asks

"We are by the bathrooms at the boathouse," Cecilia says calmly.

"Ya'll be safe, you need someone else to come be with you?" Sasha asks.

"We're OK. Your brothers are here with us" Cecilia says with confidence.

"Oh, OK, very cool. Keep on with your idea. Sasha out."

"10–4 Green Rhino!"

There is a pause while the others take in the new information.

"Mr. Lazarus may be the teacher Chief Charley was talking about." Wu is the first to say what all of them are thinking.

"That could be one answer," Stacy says petting Tabitha in her lap.

"Does anyone know what a Sadducee is?" Izaak asks glancing at Chad. Chad shakes his head.

"I think it's from the Bible. I remember hearing the word around Easter time," Sasha says.

"Chad is only a small part Jewish on his dad's side, but that word sounds Bibley to me also," Stacy chimes in.

"Ya'll got a dictionary in here?" Wu asks.

"No," Izaak says, "but I bet Izzy knows what Sadducee means."

"Probably, but let's let her and Cecilia do their thing first," Sasha says.

"Hey, does any of this mystery stuff have anything to do with Zoltar being missing?" Rich says, sounding a little scared. Stacy reaches over and holds his hand.

There is silence until Sasha senses it and says, "We don't know, but I bet Zoltar is just doing something with his family. I didn't see anyone but cousins at the booth."

"Oh yeah, that's right," Rich says reassuring himself.

Sasha and Stacy connect with their eyes. They seem to be good at leading this group without Dom around.

"I think we are all tired, I know I am!" Sasha says, "how about we call Izzy and Cecilia and call it a night."

"What about Tulpen?" Izaak asks with a full belly.

Chad looks at him with confidence.

"Me and Chad can keep first watch from the crow's nest," Izaak says. "You can see right into Dom's room from there."

"Chad, go grab some Orange Crush from the cooler in our shed. That'll keep ya up all night," Stacy says with a tactical voice.

"The rest of ya'll get some sleep. Then me and Wu can watch in the morning," Sasha decisively says.

Wu nods a big yes to the plan.

The walkie crackles again.

"Hey, Sasha," Izzy says excitedly.

"We are here," Sasha walkies back.

"We split up for a bit, and Mr. Lazarus tried following Cecilia, then he saw me and tried to follow me, then out of nowhere Mr. Fremont tried to pick a fight with him, but he is waaay too drunk to throw a punch. Weird, huh? Izzy over."

"What are they doing now?" Sasha asks.

"Cops broke it up, and Mr. Lazarus left. Izzy over."

Sasha holds up the walkie for input from the others. Nobody responds—too tired.

"Hey Izzy, we are wrapping it up here. Ya'll enjoy the concert, and we'll see you tomorrow. Sasha out."

Founders Day 1973 ends.

6

I JUST WANNA BE A DUCK

Stacy's Dream:
Flying over a wind-blown cornfield.
The stalks are high and full.
A high rise apartment building 40 stories high;
the clouds fly past in the opposite direction.
A burning bush in a courtyard
Stacy enters the dream wearing Dom's jersey but she is an adult.
Cables and chords snake their way to a table.
Dom is standing next to the table, arms crossed and wearing the No.
37 jersey,
But he is older—looks like a grown man. She walks up to him.
Blinding light
A whispered voice: Do not be afraid.

Stacy wakes up and is frustrated. Tabitha stirs at her side. Her dream has only added the one new piece where Dom is in the room also. He is all grown up. What does it mean? She can usually get more clarity when she wears a personal item. The first time she saw Dom in a dream, it was the dream telling her to come earlier to Mistletoe. He was sitting on the picnic table behind the basketball goal. Tulpen was on the table in front of him all laid out and purring. The whole dream was Tulpen's purring. Dom was waving to Stacy to come to the table. In the dream she was slowly coming to the table. She woke from that dream every day for a month, but he was his present age in the dream. He was saying something to her while he waved to her. Finally, two weeks before the move, she could hear what he was saying, "Founders Day." She talked the families into moving earlier to get here for Founders Day, and she still hasn't met him. It seems like moving early was important with all that happened with Chief Charley. But why has she met everybody but Dom? And Zoltar—where is he? She senses he is OK, but Rich is so worried.

This new dream is different. Three days in a row, but nothing revealing about it or connecting it to Chief Charley's visions.

Her mission today is to meet Dom. Chad is starting to give her the hairy eyeball for wearing Dom's jersey under her other shirt all the time. Sasha too, wonders what that is about. He came home with his family late Monday night after the Founders Day holiday. Everybody was wiped out on Monday, and then by lunch, word spread quickly on KTOE that Chief Charley had died Sunday night. It appears he passed over soon after the kids visited him. He was found dead but peaceful in his rocking chair. With the news, all the kids freaked out and stayed at home. Vacation Bible School at Redeemer where Sasha goes was even cancelled for Monday and Tuesday. There was a public viewing at the Mistletoe Auditorium. It was a huge deal to be there and walk past Chief Charley.

It's now Wednesday, and life in Mistletoe should get back to normal. Chief Charley's body is being escorted back to the Black Hills for his funeral pyre. Stacy's mom and Chad's mom are talking about going. The only constant with the group has been the security rotations, watching Tulpen. Everybody has taken a shift, and Sasha has kept one walkie talkie in charge of communications. Sasha can see right into Dom's room when she is there, but Tulpen also likes to wander the block in the wee hours. Sasha loves to tell the story of Chad and Izaak trying to hide while following Tulpen around the neighborhood.

Stacy gets up out of bed and takes the jersey off and tosses it onto the bed. She heads into the bathroom in the hall, just as Luke is getting out. She needs a shower before heading to Vacation Bible School at Redeemer LCMS at the end of Lake street.

Sasha is waiting before the opening of VBS at Redeemer Church at the entrance of the school side of Redeemer on the outside staircase halfway up on the landing. This is where she instructed the others to meet her and get the itinerary for the day. They have not all met since Sunday night. They are up to four walkie talkies now. Redeemer is Sasha's church. She is the only one in her family to go here. Her brothers went to the Redeemer school before her, but the Quinterro family has remained Catholic. The Catholic school on Church row near Mistletoe closed in the '50s, and the Quinterros didn't want to send Sasha to the other Catholic school in downtown San Antonio. She started at Redeemer Lutheran in kindergarten and liked it. She likes that it is her school. Deacon comes to school and church here with his dad. Dom and his mom go to Pleasant Valley Lutheran. Sasha found out at the barbeque that the Stones and Simms families will be joining Redeemer. This makes Sasha very happy. She relishes the idea of being a host.

It's about half an hour until VBS starts and Izaak has checked in. Tulpen is sleeping at the Blue house on Dom's bed. Izaak decided to close the window in Dom's room and close his bedroom door. No one will be around for a couple hours to keep watch. Dom doesn't know about the latest visions of the Chief. He is still sad at his passing. Sasha has instructed the others to let her catch Dom up on everything.

Stacy, Wu, Izzy and Cecilia ride up on their bikes and park. Stacy rides with Izzy. Sasha rushes up and is a bit flummoxed, "Where are the boys? They coming up behind ya'll? It's almost time to start VBS."

"Hello to you too, Bosha!" Wu says in that mocking tone she hopes Sasha catches, but she does not react in too harsh a manner.

Sasha raises up, folds her arms, looks mad, but then breathes in heavily like she is about to hyperventilate, catches her mood, redirects, "Yes, hello."

All four ladies take a calm breath and then Stacy puts a gentle hand on Sasha's shoulder. She chimes in, "Dom is hanging with Rich. He wanted to go by Zoltar's house and sniff around. He also mentioned a boy named Toby?"

"Toby fixes bikes," Izzy says to Stacy.

"Oh," Stacy acknowledges.

"What about the others, Chad and Izaak?" Sasha asks nearing a tizzy state.

"They took care of Tulpen and then joined Rich and Dom," Wu says calmly.

Izzy notices that things tend to get calmer when Stacy puts her hand on someone's shoulder. She files that information away to share another time.

Stacy looks right at her at that moment of thought.

Izzy glances back and sort of knows that Stacy just read her mind but shrugs it off.

"OK, I got an idea," Sasha states gently and motions all the girls toward the playground.

"I need to talk to Dom today, but I guess it can wait," Sasha says as she walks.

"Me too," Stacy says. She walks step for step next to her.

Sasha smiles at her and huddles up the crew on the merry go round that is covered with rocks. Wu starts to wipe them off, but Sasha stops her. "We need these."

Sasha begins to outline the upstairs floor of the school where VBS will take place. She maps out the fifth-grade room, the library and the fourth-grade room and so on.

"Empty your pockets, ladies," Sasha says in full planning mode.

Wu's gum pack becomes a water cooler.

Izzy's bookmarks become the girls' and boys' bathrooms at the end of the hall.

Stacy's ABA basketball schedule from Lakota becomes the stairs to the hallway.

Each of them have various barrettes from their hair that become different key people like teachers and even the janitor.

Once the whole area is laid out just like Sasha imagines, she shows the girls the movement of the plan.

"After the first snack, our fourth-grade group will walk from here to here, heading back to our room."

"But we are fifth graders!" Wu states defiantly.

"When school starts yes, but VBS goes by your last grade," Sasha states.

"Oh," Wu says.

"Before we get to the classroom, Wu will sneak off to the library to look up the word Sadducee " Sasha continues.

"Why not Izzy; she's better at looking up stuff?" Wu asks.

"Stacy and Wu both have the black hair. We have to confuse Mrs. Martin, the teacher, into thinking Stacy is Wu. Stacy, you are actually going to hide out until snack time and then sneak up to join the group when Wu breaks off from the group."

"Mrs. Martin will notice that!" Izzy says.

Sasha smiles and pulls out a pair of glasses from her pocket.

"Got that covered." Sasha says confidently. "I am going to switch out Mrs. Martin's glasses with her old ones. I snaked this pair from the Lions Club recycle box. These are her old ones and just a bit fuzzy for her."

"But what about my feathers?" Stacy asks.

"Got that covered too!" Sasha says as she reaches into her bag and pulls out clip-on feathers for each girl. Izzy gets green, Cecilia gets blue, and Sasha gets red. She even has a spare set of lilac for Wu.

The plan is all set, and the church chimes start ringing eight times for the start of VBS.

Meanwhile at Toby Windwalker's Bike Shed, the boys walk up to the shed that was open and see Toby working on a three-speed, banana-seat bike with a really extra-long fork to the front wheel.

They stop and watch for a bit. Toby is very intent on securing the front wheel. He cranks one last turn on the nut and then jumps up excited. He sees the boys and waves but doesn't hesitate. He hops on the bike and pedals out and around the boys with a huge grin on his face. The long front end of the bike is twice the size of the actual frame or torso of the rest of the bike. Toby wheels into the street and circles a few times, trying to maneuver the big turning radius. After a few passes, he pulls up to the guys.

"She doesn't turn too good, and she's *not* fast, but doesn't she look cool?" Toby says as he sits proudly on his new creation.

"Why, she?" Dom asks.

"Hey, Toby," Rich says happily.

"Very cool," Izaak adds.

You can see Izaak's eyes pouring over the design and making mental treehouse notes in his head for future reference.

Dom chats with Toby. Rich looks around the shed and notices Zoltar's bike is in the side where Toby keeps bikes he hasn't gotten to yet. He walks over to double-check his suspicions and sees the Tackle Ball stickers on the middle part of the frame, as well as Rams and Steelers helmets and a faded Rhino's logo.

"Hey, Toby," Rich calls out. "Is this Zoltar's bike?"

"Yeah, he left it here for a tune up," Toby calls back.

Rich turns to Toby excited, "When did he leave it?"

"Last week, I think. He said he was gonna be gone for a while and said I could trick it out a bit like a low rider bike for next year's Cinco de Mayo parade."

"Did he say when he was coming back?" Rich asks.

"Nah, but the whole family is there; you can ask them. It's a full house next door. Toby says and dismounts his new project and wheels it into the shed.

"Any of you guys speak Spanish?" Toby asks.

The guys look around at each other and then Chad nods and slowly walks over to the house next door.

There is a chain-link fence around the whole house, even up to the front sidewalk here on Magnolia Street. Dogs are usually barking like crazy, and there are chickens all over. The Gomez's own this house and the house behind them to the next block on Huisache Street. This is one of the few blocks in Mistletoe that doesn't have an alley between blocks for trash pickup. The fence goes all the way back to the front yard behind them on the next street. They have lots of chickens. Chad walks up to the gate and walks through with no problem. He knocks on the door and immediately dogs bark in the house and from the shed in the back. The shed dogs come running up to attack Chad. He calmly puts out his hand and the dogs sniff him and walk away. The door opens, and the inside dogs are chomping at the screen door and a short lady answers in Spanish. The other boys try to listen, but Chad's back is to them. After a polite conversation, the lady smiles and waves to Chad. The dogs stop barking, and Chad comes back over.

"So, where's Zoltar? When's he getting back?" Rich says at almost panicky level.

"The Gomez family is gone for the summer," Chad says calmly while he takes out a stick of gum from his pocket.

"Well, who are those guys?" Dom asks.

"The Gomez family," Chad says chewing his new gum.

Rich looks at Dom and Izaak with a very exacerbated look.

"Zoltar's got lots of cousins and aunts and uncles," Izaak says with a mocking smile at Rich.

"And an abuela," Chad says and puts his hands in his pocket.

Before Rich can ask, Dom says "A grandmother."

Rich storms off in a huff with no new knowledge.

The boys follow, and they head back to the treehouse through the path by Sasha's house.

Back at VBS, the four girls go into the church for the opening of VBS. The church is next to the school. Stacy hangs back and watches from the back row while all the different grades get into their groups. At the front of the church, Pastor Neil holds a mic and welcomes everybody. He is new to Redeemer since May, and this is his first church. He has shoulder-length shaggy blonde hair and looks a bit like Jesus.

"Welcome everybody to Redeemer and our neighborhood Vacation Bible School!"

The kids and teacher clap in applause.

"I would like to get us started with a song everybody knows. I am new here and just learning the ropes!"

"Where ya from?" one of the adults asks.

"Illinois!" he says with minimal response from the crowd.

"OK, a song" he restarts. "This is my daughter Ringo, she'll be an eighth grader this year. 'Jesus loves you.'"

Pastor Neil sets the mic on the stand in front of his daughter. She is sitting on a folding chair with a guitar and the longest braided ponytail anyone has ever seen.

"This is a song everyone should know, just a little funkier." She looks up to her dad.

Pastor Neil starts clapping, one, two, three, stop. He repeats it—one, two, three, claps, stop. He is starting a beat. The crowd follows.

Ringo strums heavy and along with the beat. We can hear her guitar without a mic. She calls out the first "Jesus Loves You" chorus and waits for response.

The song goes over well. Cecilia is particularly juiced by this version and stands in her row the whole time. Eventually everyone is standing through this new, funkier version of "Jesus Loves You."

After the opening, the groups are supposed to go to their own rooms, but Cecilia goes up front to talk to Ringo. The others instinctively follow. "Where did you learn to play so well?" Cecilia gushes to Ringo as she stands up.

"Our home church in Illinois" Ringo says happily. "My mom and her best friend were a folksy duo and taught me on a banjo when I was four."

Pastor Neil is standing behind them beaming like a proud papa.

"My dad got me a ukulele, and I just about got it figured out," Cecilia says excitedly.

Ringo smiles and goes behind the altar and brings out her own ukulele to show Cecilia. She hands it to her, "What can you play?"

Cecilia starts to play as Mrs. Martin comes up to collect her wayward class. Stacy has also wandered up the side of the church to try to hear what's going on.

"Come along, ladies, class is this way," Mrs. Martin says with that smarmy teacher voice that drips disapproval.

"Oh, sorry," Cecilia hands the ukulele back to Ringo. "Can you teach me some chords?" she calls back to Ringo.

Ringo looks at her dad.

Pastor Neil steps up, "We will be here all day after VBS if you ladies can stay for a bit."

"It's ya'll, Dad. Get with the lingo—we're in Texas now!" Ringo gently scolds her dad.

He gives her a return look, "Why yes, I reckon ya'll can set a spell after lunch."

Everybody but Mrs. Martin laughs.

Stacy steps up and joins in the conversation, startling Mrs. Martin who is now grabbing for Izzy's hand to lead the group away.

"Maybe Pastor Neil can help us with that library thing," Stacy says and gets a stern look from Sasha.

"What library thing?" Pastor Neil asks very happily.

Sasha grabs Stacy and Wu, and Cecilia follows. Izzy is trapped by Mrs. Martin, and they all head down the altar steps and away to class.

"We'll stop by after VBS," Cecilia calls back. Ringo and her dad look dumbfounded on the altar steps.

The group of girls catches up to the rest of their class, and Sasha gets up next to Stacy and loud whispers at her.

"We *have* a plan" she says fiercely.

"I saw an opening with the guitar girl, and I went for it" Stacy says calmly back at Sasha.

The group is caught up and waiting now behind the big group.

Sasha and Stacy lock eyes.

"I am sorry, boss lady, but that plan was too much to take in at 7:45 a.m." She looks to the others for help.

Wu nods and so does Izzy.

"Yeah, a bit … complicated without my morning Dr. Pepper," Cecilia chimes in, wary of Sasha's response.

Stacy puts a hand on Sasha's shoulder while looking at Izzy. "I am *not* trying to take over from your fair leadership, Miss Bosha," Stacy starts to explain. The word Bosha gets a gasp from the other girls. Sasha doesn't like the word Bosha from anyone outside the group. "Next time I will try to consult before going off plan, but I saw something in this girl Ringo, and it would be cool to get other new folks into a good standing, don't ya think? Besides, Cecilia has already bonded with Ringo, and her dad certainly knows what a Sadducee is."

"You're right," Sasha says without pause.

Another gasp!

"This will be easier to do after VBS, and we can all chill and have fun." Sasha says. The lines start moving into the school.

Stacy grips Sasha's shoulder a little bit harder but still gently.

Sasha looks into her eyes.

"I will always be with you, never against you" Stacy says very sincerely.

Sasha nods yes and quietly says "OK" while still caught in Stacy's gaze. Stacy releases her and looks to Izzy with a knowing smile.

Izzy tries not to think anything.

At the treehouse, the four boys are sprawled out around the main room of the sycamore treehouse. Chad is taking his first look around this well-designed fortress. Izaak grabs a comic book right away. Dom tries spinning the ABA ball on his finger. Rich is still disturbed, and after some thoughtful thinking, he speaks up.

"Why wouldn't Zoltar tell us he was leaving? I don't get it. That last night we were talking all night. Nothing ever came up about him leaving."

The ABA ball spins off Dom's finger and rolls over to Chad. Chad picks it up instinctively and spins it perfectly on his middle finger, then transfers it to his ring finger. It keeps spinning, then he switches hands effortlessly. He uses his free hand to keep it spinning, slapping the ball without knocking it off.

Dom and Rich just stare at him. *This one has many talents* is the thought that crosses their shared stares.

"He's not gone forever!" Dom says reassuringly.

Rich looks relieved, then looks at Chad for a sign of confirmation since he spoke to the abuela.

Chad shakes his head no, without even looking at the spinning ball.

Izaak speaks up from behind his Silver Surfer No. 37, "Didn't some of his cousins leave last summer to go work on a farm somewhere out in California?"

"Yeah!" Dom jumps on that thought. "I bet that's what happened. The Gomez family is huge, and they are always helping each other do stuff. That's got to be it."

Rich is smiling now. He starts to nod his head with the idea. "Yeah, let's go with that. Besides, Stacy said she senses he is OK. She seems to sense things and like, know things." At that moment Chad knocks the ball off his finger, and it bounces over and into the comic box, perfectly.

Chad looks at the boys with a quirky smile, like it was supposed to happen that way.

Dom and Rich take in the slightly weird vibe, and then Izaak breaks the mood. He puts down his comic book, "Let's play some 21!" He grabs the still-moving ball from the comic book milk crate and heads down to the court. The others follow gladly.

Back at VBS, the day's classes are over, and the whole group of 150 or so are collected into the upstairs loft next to the basketball court in the gym at the school. Lutherans love to eat. The lunch area of the school is full, and kids and adults are enjoying sandwiches, cookies, and orange slices. Cups of Kool-Aid are being refilled by the nice church ladies. The five girls are huddled together with Ringo at a table. Mr. Lazarus is one table over, and Stacy keeps an eye on him for reasons yet unknown. She can stare his way, but he cannot see her looking at him.

Pastor Neil stops by toward the end of lunch and invites the ladies to come by his office in the back of the church where Ringo has moved her guitars and other instruments. Mr. Lazarus gets up and introduces himself to Pastor. Ringo gets the girls to clean up their lunch stuff, and then they start heading to the stairs and over to the church. Stacy looks back and catches Mr. Lazarus looking at her.

Ringo opens the door to a spacious office that is nestled into the back corner of one of the offshoots of the church. The whole church is in the shape of a basic cross. The first thing you notice when you walk into the space is the big circular stained-glass window behind the desk. You can see the ivy on the outside covering the top third of the window. There aren't any lights on as the natural light fills the office with a gentle glow. Wu is most impressed with this moment. She would say years later that visiting Pastor Neil's office that first time was what inspired her to be a pastor.

There is a couch where Cecilia and Ringo sit and pick up the guitar and ukulele. Izzy and Wu check out the two full walls of books on either side. Sasha and Stacy each take to the two solo comfy chairs.

After about fifteen minutes Pastor Neil and Mr. Lazarus enter the office laughing heartily like old college roommates. They all look up.

"Ladies, this is Mr. Lazarus. He will be your fifth-grade teacher for English and science at the school this next year," Pastor says and catches his breath from an obviously vigorous conversation.

"Oh, hey, I didn't catch your first name," Pastor asks Mr. Lazarus.

"Mr. Lazarus will do," he says with his hands behind his back in a formal manner.

"Oh, yes, right … well, ladies, I remember a question about the library?"

Sasha and Stacy look at each other.

Izzy speaks up from the one bookshelf and without turning to look, "Yes, Pastor, we were curious about the Sadducees," she says with her usual knowledgeable authority. It is known within this group of ladies that Izzy is the smartest and most well-read. Wu easily agrees.

Pastor is taken a bit back. Mr. Lazarus's eyebrow perks up like Mr. Spock from Star Trek.

"Heady stuff" he says and walks to the other side of his shelves where Wu has found an interesting magazine. "Right here," Pastor collects a dusty copy from the top shelf. Izzy is quick beside him with curiosity.

Pastor takes the book behind his desk and opens it up looking for something specific. He motions that its ok for Izzy to join him.

"The Sadducees and Pharisees were the religious and political leaders of the Temple in Jesus's day. They were part of the Jewish story from the Old Testament, and they were always questioning Jesus during his ministry in the New Testament," he says and then looks up.

Izzy is the only one of the girls who doesn't seem dumbfounded.

"Wasn't there a song?" Izzy asks very studiously.

"A song?" Pastor asks. Mr. Lazarus's other eyebrow goes up this time.

"Yes," Izzy says. "I think I heard it at camp. I don't wanna be a ..."

Pastor finishes the line. "Sad-du-cee, because they're so sad you see!"

There is a pause of amazement at the connection between Pastor and Izzy.

Ringo instinctively picks up the tune. Cecilia stops and watches Ringo's fingers move.

Pastor and Izzy repeat the line together.

"I don't wanna be a Sad-du-cee ... Because they're so sad you see ..."

They look at the others to join in.

Ringo keeps time and leads them. Cecilia starts to strum gently on the ukulele while watching Ringo change chords.

All together, they sang, "I don't wanna be a Sad-du-cee, because they're so sad you see." The group is getting into it then pauses for the next line.

Mr. Lazarus chimes in, "I don't wanna be a Pharisee, because they're not fair you see!" he sings heartily.

Everybody joins in ... two more times with the Pharisee.

Then they paused, waiting for another line.

Pastor puts down his book and starts flapping his arms.

"I just wanna be a Duck, Quack Quack" he moves around the room delighting the girls with his silliness.

"I just wanna be a duck ... " He waits for the others to quack with him.

"quack, quack ..."

Pastor laughs and laughs and then heads back to his desk.

Wu is sitting at the desk and looking at an illustration in the book Pastor got from the shelf. She points at the picture.

"What is this symbol" Wu asks, as the mood of the room calms down.

Pastor stands next to her in his chair.

"That's the star of David, a common symbol for the Jewish faith and heritage."

"Is this all of it?" She asks with a very serious look on her face.

"All of it?" Pastor asks, a bit confused.

"Yes," she looks up at him and around at the others who have her entire attention.

"I have seen this symbol before, but with an X inside the star.

"On who," Mr. Lazarus asks immediately.

"Who?" Pastor asks, "Don't you mean where?"

"No, he means who," Stacy chimes in. "I have seen it before also." She looks to Wu as if to back up her seemingly silly proclamation.

Stacy has seen the symbol in an old dream, maybe even last year. The star was in flames. She only had it once but doesn't feel safe yet, sharing the details out loud. Izzy looks at Stacy like before.

Izzy speaks up, "I have seen it also, but in a dream I had."

"With the X?" Wu asks.

"Who did you see this symbol on?" Mr. Lazarus asks more emphatically.

"Mr. Fremont," Wu says.

"Mr. Fremont?" Sasha asks very questionably.

"Yes," she says and lays her hands across the desk, searching her mind for the story.

"Cecilia and I were there," Wu says

"Me?" Cecilia asks, not really wanting to be in this story.

"It was you, me, Izaak, and your dad," Wu continues and looks to

Cecilia for confirmation, but Cecilia gave no response.

"Mr. Fremont was drunk and passed out on his front lawn, No. 2103. We were doing rounds for your dad. We watched him for a while."

"Last year, Founders Day!" Cecilia remembers.

"We didn't want to get too close, and your dad was already asleep" Cecilia jumps in, "He started to puke, and he was on his back"

Wu continues, "We tried to roll him over, but he was too heavy."

"So we kicked him in the butt, like four times to wake him up," Cecilia says.

"He half wakes up and rolls over and pukes into the grass," Wu says.

"And that's when I saw the tattoo on his neck, on the back. It was this symbol but with an X in the middle. I only saw it cause he had a ponytail. He never wore a ponytail," Wu finishes the story.

Mr. Lazarus doesn't say a word and hastily leaves.

Everyone is silent, wondering what just happened.

The girls all throw glances at each other, wondering if this has anything to do with Chief Charley's visions. It feels weird that they would all have the same thought at once. Ringo and her dad look at each other, not really knowing what is going on.

Pastor Neil breaks the silence, "Well, that was interesting"

7

RHINOS AND TWO LIPS

The walkie in Sasha's pocket crackles, " Hey, Bosha, you there? over."

"Don't call me that, over." Sasha responds.

"Where ya 'at? over." Izaak chirps.

"We are just leaving the church; big things going on, over," Sasha says very boss like.

"Oh,"

then a pause,

"over,"

then another pause. "This is Izaak."

"I know who you are, doofus, over."

The girls are huddled over their bikes, except for Cecilia who is still over by the church, chatting with Ringo.

The walkie is left on and we can hear the boys arguing over something.

The girls listen and smile at each other.

"All right, all right … what? … yeah, yeah … I *know!*" Izaak still has his button on the open line. "Hey, Chad says his mom can make more of those great sandwiches, ya'll coming over? over."

"We already ate, over," Sasha says not hesitating.

"We're playing basketball, over," Izaak says with a little bit of persuasion in his voice.

"On our way," Sasha says and keeps the button on an open channel. She yells over to Cecilia, "Basketball! Bring Ringo."

"What's a Ringo? over," Izaak asks from the other end.

Sasha doesn't respond to Izaak.

"Hey, how did she get the Beatle name?" she asks Wu and Stacy and Izzy.

The girls ride up and into the block from church. Ringo is riding Wu's bike with her ukulele in the basket. Izzy is standing on pedals and riding her bike with Wu on the seat behind her. Wu didn't have the strength to give Ringo a pump on her bike. Stacy is riding with Sasha. They all ride right through the game, halting play. Sasha has a big, toothy grin, leading the girls on an obvious attempt to make an entrance. The boys don't even gripe. She does this all the time.

Sasha ditches her bike with Stacy and comes over, dictating a new game. She is clapping loudly as she walks over and grabs the ball.

"OK, me, Dom, Izzy, Rich, and Stacy," she calls out.

"Not me. Ya'll play; I'll watch," Stacy calls back to the group.

"OK, Izaak, Wu, Chad, Cecilia, and Ringo"

"I'm good, not my thing. I'll keep … Stacy? company." Ringo says checking with Stacy that she got the name right. Stacy nods, and they sit on the picnic table that is back behind the goalpost.

"Oh no," Dom says loudly, complaining, "No brother–sister cheating, no sir."

"I'll switch with Cecilia, but I only got half an hour until I have to mow," Izzy says and grabs the ball and shoots.

"Mowing!" Dom complains "You DaVincis are always mowing!"

"Then I suggest you shut up and we play." Izzy snipes back at him.

Rich calls over to Stacy, "Hey, can you grab that crate of jerseys from the treehouse? Izaak always gripes when he passes to the wrong team. We need green and gray sides." Stacy nods and motions Ringo to go up with her and check out the treehouse.

The girls start shooting and warming up. The boys go get a drink from the hose in Dom's yard.

Stacy yells to Chad to catch the laundry bag full of jerseys. Stacy shows Ringo the main landing with Tulpen purring on Dom's pillow.

Chad holds open the bag and everybody gets out their favorite number on reversable jerseys. Favorite numbers are important.

"We get green," Sasha says without any argument from the gray team.

Izzy gets No. 32 for Dr. J.

Izaak gets No. 8, his baseball number for Yogi Berra.

Rich gets out No. 4 since he is Mistletoe, the IV.

Cecilia gets out No. 33 for Kareem.

Wu gets No. 00 for Jeff Chao, the Asian Wilt Chamberlin.

Chad gets No. 13, the spare jersey.

Sasha gets No. 31 because that is her number.

Dom looks around for No. 37, but it's not in the bag. He has to settle for No. 55, Zoltar's oversize jersey.

"Hey, where's my jersey" he complains, but the game has started.

Stacy hears this and looks out the window of the treehouse. Rich sees her and smiles.

"I think Tulpen got it all ..." he searches for the right word, "fuzzy. I had to wash it for ya, ya whiny excuse for a point guard."

"I can't wear this thing! I look like I'm wearing a painting smock from kindergarten," Dom complains to no avail, his arms outstretched and swallowed whole by Zoltar's massive essence.

The game commences, and the two teams play like old friends showing a new guy how they do it. Chad, the new guy, has already shown his worth as a set-up guy; picks, screens, and rebounds are his game. He helps Wu the most as he sets picks on Dom who tries to guard the speedy Wu. Izzy and Izaak have played very well together. They are the two tallest of the bunch, and they easily beat Sasha's green team.

Stacy and Ringo keep exploring; they go up to the crow's nest for the view, then climb back down to watch. Soon after they sit on top of the picnic table, and Ringo starts to strum a Beatles song on her ukulele. They notice Steve Hamilton on his porch with his grandma. Grandma Hamilton is smoking her pipe, and Steve can't take his eyes off Ringo. Wu notices and gets Sasha's attention. They both notice Steve's newfound interest in the kids of the block. They have got to get a better name for the group. Steve is also a thirteen-year-old like Ringo. Sasha gives Wu the eye, and they both share a matchmaking idea for later.

"Hey, Ringo," Stacy begins to ask, "how did you get your cool name?"

"I was wondering how long it would take before one of you guys asked me that," she says and keeps strumming what sounds like

"Octopus's Garden."

"I think we have to say ya'll now that we are in Texas," Stacy says with a smile. "I am new to this town also."

"I like it here. People are really friendly," Ringo says to Stacy.

Stacy remains quiet waiting for an answer.

"Oh yeah, my mom was from Liverpool. She actually knew the Beatles. She and Dad met there when Dad was an exchange student. She named me after Ringo, even before he joined the Beatles. I was almost named Rory Storm!" she says and stops strumming. "Mom was fifteen when she had me; Dad was sixteen. Dad brought us home to Illinois while he was still in school before VSC. My grandparents helped raise me and Mom!"

Stacy smiles and seems very intent on Ringo's story.

"You're very easy to talk to. I haven't told anyone that about my mom and dad." Ringo says and feels Stacy's calmness.

"Dad is always worried the church may not understand how much in love they were at such a young age, but then he always says that the Virgin Mary was like fourteen, probably when she had Jesus!" Stacy's eyes get big!

"He gets in trouble for saying that too!" Ringo says, and they both laugh.

The game ends on an Izzy long shot, and she runs off to her bike, "Gotta go, guys."

Stacy looks at Ringo, "you play?"

"Oh, no," Ringo says and begins to strum hard, launching into a full version of the Octopus, "music is my thing."

Stacy yells at the group of seven, "I'm in."

Chad smiles because he knows what's coming.

She takes off her top to reveal Dom's No. 37 underneath her oversized black t-shirt. She grabs the ball, and Sasha starts to guard her. She dribbles between her skirt and puts her black Chuck Taylors to speed overdrive and flies past Sasha for a layup, and she slaps the backboard for effect, showing her jumping skills.

"Damn!" Sasha says with respect.

After a third game in the heat, the group starts to lag a bit. Wu mentions the pool. This idea is met with great exuberance.

Before Stacy and Chad can walk off to get their suits, Rich catches them both, "Hey, can ya'll come with me before the pool? I got something to show you." Rich has worked up enough nerve to talk to Stacy. He would rather do this without Chad around, but he always seems to be with her, so he invites him along also.

"Sure," Stacy looks over to see that Sasha has already corralled Dom for a talk. "Hey, ya'll going to the pool?" Stacy yells over to Dom and Sasha. "Yeah, we'll get there," Sasha calls back

Dom doesn't flinch, sensing Sasha needs to bend his ear.

Stacy looks at Chad and nods. He walks away and back to his house.

"See ya at the pool," Stacy calls back.

Chad hears this with his back to Stacy. He stops and turns around and stares back at her.

Stacy stares back confused. They lock eyes. "Oh, hey, Rich, where is the pool?"

"Other end of Woodlawn Lake from here," Rich says.

Chad turns around and heads into his house.

"Do I need my suit?" Stacy asks.

"No, we can swing back by here," Rich says.

"Where are we going?" Stacy asks with her hands behind her back. She sways back and forth, wondering what adventure Rich has for her.

"Gotta see a man about a horse" Rich says all grown up like. He doesn't realize he is mixing his metaphors.

"We're going to the bathroom?" Stacy looks confused. "My dad says that every time he gets up from his lazy boy."

Rich turns red, "Uh ... no, here follow me," He takes Stacy by the hand, and they walk the pathway by the creek next to Sasha's house and head over to Toby's.

They pass by Dom and Sasha who are behind their two houses and in the creek with their shoes off. They are building a dam.

Stacy passes by and hopes she can talk to Dom alone very soon.

Sasha doesn't even see Rich and Stacy walk by. She is busy telling him about all of the things he has missed since Founders Day. She catches him up on the visit with Chief Charley before he died. She tells him about the Tulpen watch and why he has found Tulpen locked up in his room several times. She then tells him about how she and the girls met Mr. Lazarus today and how he got all spooked when the Sadducee thing came up. She wonders what old man Fremont has got to do with any of this. Dom listens carefully to all of it and then sits on his pile of rocks, thinking. He takes a good long five minutes. The slow sounds of creek movement are calming. Sasha keeps quiet. Dom takes it all in, then bolts his head up and asks," So … why is Stacy wearing my Rhino's jersey?"

Sasha ponders this," I don't know."

"Stacy's kinda weird, but not in a bad way," he says.

Sasha thinks on that for a bit. "Yeah, she has this touching thing that makes things all slow and calm and … Peaceful."

"Yeah!" Dom says with a look that says Sasha hit the point right on the nose.

"Why do you think that is?" he asks.

They ponder that and add a few more rocks to the small dam they have constructed.

"I don't know," Sasha says, and it is hard for her to say so. Sasha prides herself on leading this group. It is hard for her to honestly admit that she doesn't know.

It's quiet again.

"Hey, Dom," Sasha asks calmly.

"Yeah, Sasha," he replies.

"Stacy wants to talk to you alone. I think it's important to her," she says.

He takes this in and continues to ponder the rocks.

He looks up to Sasha.

"I think at the Rhino's game tonight," she says.

"Can I get my jersey back?" he says very seriously.

Sasha just smiles at him.

Rich and Stacy arrive at Toby's. He is still holding her hand. She looks up at him to see what his next move will be at this interesting but confusing destination.

"This is Toby Windwalker's Bike Shed. He and his older sisters supply bikes for everybody in Mistletoe." He says and decides to continue holding her hand as long as she will let him. She can see into the shed and see Toby working on that same long front wheel bike he showed the guys this morning.

"So where are the sisters?" Stacy asks.

Rich is looking into those amazing violet eyes.

"Huh?" his mouth stumbles.

"The sisters?" she says again

"Oh, they ride around all day showing off bikes that Toby has fixed up. They sell them to people and drum up repair business. They are older, in high school. They just started going outside the walls and into San Antonio." He says without taking his eyes away from her light purple gaze.

Toby walks up and breaks the connection.

"Twice in one day from the Rich man. What's up?" Toby announces while he wipes his hands with a shop rag.

He extends his hands to Stacy, "Howdy, Toby Windwalker, horse trader." He introduces himself to Stacy. She extends her right hand. Rich still has her left hand. Toby shakes her hand and acknowledges Rich's consistent touch with Stacy.

Rich drops her hand and reaches out to Toby, acting a little more grown up than usual.

"Hey, Toby," Rich shakes Toby's hand like a businessman sealing a million-dollar deal.

"Look at you, all acting like a high school stud!" Toby says. Rich blushes.

Toby looks at Stacy and says, "What can Toby do for you today?"

Rich pipes in with a big grin on his face, "Miss Stacy needs a new ride."

"A bicycle!" Stacy says with excitement.

"Yes, why don't you have one?" Rich asks.

"I can never find an all-black one that works with my skirt. I am very particular," she says. "Besides I always ride with Chad."

"Who is Chad?" Toby asks, surprised.

"Aww, you need your own horse, Miss Stacy, don't ya think?" Rich cuts in, not wanting Stacy to answer that last question.

"Okay, let's see what Mr. Toby has for a very spoiled girl like me." She walks quickly into the shed and starts looking at his selection.

Toby and Rich watch her. Her skirt dances with the same delight as a girl picking out a new present. She looks at each one carefully and takes her time. Toby and Rich just watch and wait, not saying a word. After about fifteen solid minutes, Stacy rolls out an old-style Schwinn from the early '60s. It is a girl's bike and has plenty of room for her skirt to fit and not get caught in the chain. It is a bit rusty and faded red.

"Looks great!" Rich says happily.

"You say that now, but wait," she says coyly while holding the bike proudly next to her.

"I saw a spray painter in there. Can you make it black?" she asks Toby. He nods.

"I mean like shiny black, black as the night sky with no moon. Pitch black with stars all over."

Toby nods again.

"Can I have purple streamers on the handle bar?"

Still nodding.

"A lilac purple seat to match my eyes?"

Toby looks at Rich for a response. Rich looks straight ahead.

Toby nods to Stacy again, yes.

"And a new Texas license plate with Stacy on it, no 'e.' Stacy with a y?"

"Like at the border gift shop, when you came into Texas," Rich asks.

Toby puts a toothpick into his mouth and looks at Rich again.

Rich nods.

"And by Sunday?"

Toby nods no, "Give me a week."

Stacy nods. It seems her demands have all been satisfied.

She looks at the bike, then back to the boys. "How much will this set me back?" she asks as if this may nix the deal.

Rich starts to answer, and Toby cuts him off. Toby pats Rich on the back. "Rich can cover it; don't you worry your pretty little head."

Rich blushes at the truth.

Stacy looks puzzled, "Like dollars and cents, how much would a bike like this cost? Gotta be a lot?"

"Don't worry, Stacy with a 'y.' Rich owns this town."

Stacy hands the bike off to Toby and joins Rich . She extends her hand, and they walk back towards the path to the treehouse. Rich is feeling very proud. They pass the dam built by Dom and Sasha.

"Must be at the pool already," Stacy mentions.

Rich just smiles at her. He is feeling like he is on a cloud, flying and walking at the same time. When they make it to the picnic table by the treehouse, Stacy stops the movement and turns to look into Rich's eyes very deeply.

"Richard Mistletoe IV, you are a very kind boy." She has locked into his soul.

"This is very important," she says. He nods.

"I am not entirely sure why my family and Chad's family wound up here. I know now after just a few days that I was chosen to be here. I can't tell you exactly why or how that is, but I know it to be true." Rich looks puzzled but still locked into her gaze.

She holds both of his hands in front of her down low at their waist.

"I will be loyal to you forever. I can feel it now, but you must know something."

Rich looks like a zombie.

"You still with me?" She asks like this has happened before.

"Yes," Rich says very purposely.

"Chad and I were born to be together" She says and waits for a response. She can see him wince at the mention of Chad's name.

"Seriously, we were born in beds next to each other at the exact same time. It's on our birth certificates."

Rich squeezes her hands a bit harder.

"Chad and I will always be together, married, kids, the whole way. It's just how it will be. Our paths are one," she pulls their hands together for effect. She leans in and gives Rich a kiss on the cheek, "Then let's go." She heads off toward her house.

"See you at the pool," she calls back.

In the northwest corner of Mistletoe is a Texas-sized baseball stadium, literally. The Mistletoe Rhinos play AA baseball in a stadium that was built in the shape of Texas. It fits nicely just inside the St. Cloud and Babcock street corner. It is inside the Mistletoe wall but easily accessible to the San Antonio car garages. The Mistletoe elevated train that connects to downtown San Antonio goes through deep centerfield, elevated high above the outfield. The stadium seats are built around the train, and it is a big tourist attraction. Mistletoe Stadium is also used for the college and high school games. The Rhinos, however, have first dibs on use of the facility.

Mistletoe loves their Rhinos, but before that, they loved their Giraffes. The town has a tradition of renaming all of their team mascots every decade. There is a big vote in the ninth year, and then everything changes. All sports teams in the town are named after the new mascot, using different colors for the different school teams at every level. The minor league team gets first choice of new colors. Then the college, then the high school, and so on down to middle school and little league—all sports. Right now, here in 1973, the Mistletoe Rhinos are purple and red. They have a big red rhino face and horn on the front of their purple jerseys. In the '60s, they were Giraffes. They wore a green and orange jungle-looking colors, like in the grasslands of Africa. In the '50s, the Blue and Gold Seagulls were a proud franchise, winning the Texas League four times.

This year, the local paper and Big Willy from KTOE have given this particular squad a special name. The "TwoLips" are doing well in the Texas League, leading the division by five games. The left fielder and center fielder are cousins, Terry and Bill Hardson, who have the two biggest mouths in baseball. They have very loud voices and have discovered the distinct echo effect they have as an advantage in left and center from the contour of the stadium. They heckle every batter that comes up from their spots in the field. They holler from the dugout when not in the field.

The TwoLips name fits nicely. Every time an opposing batter walks, the cousins chant "Tulip" at the batter as he jogs to first. When asked why they do that, they simply reply in unison, "Real men don't walk." They never explained the tulip part of it all. The best part about the cousins is they will warm up in between innings with any kid in the front row of the stands that will toss them a ball four times. They are very fan friendly.

They also back up their play in the field. Bill has seventeen putouts at home plate, throwing from anywhere in centerfield. Terry has five. During batting practice, they wear t-shirts instead of their uniforms. The shirts have a different Rhino logo on them. The Rhino has one red and one purple tulip in its mouth. The caption reads, Real Men Don't Walk. They are destined to never make the majors. They always swing on a 3–2 count, ensuring that they never walk. Good pitchers can always get them out with their best stuff. Many times, however, the cousins hit something and make things exciting. Smart pitchers give them three intentional balls, then get them to swing at anything they throw at them.

Today, The green Rhino's little league co-ed squad of Sasha, Cecilia, Izaak, Dom, Rich, Wu, and Zoltar are coached by Mr. Black. Izzy plays volleyball. The rest of the team are other May-borns. They came in third in their division this year behind the fierce red Rhinos who won again, like last year. All the various colors of Rhinos are filing into the outfield bleachers in the early evening shade of the stadium. This is the after-season party recognizing the great youth baseball program that plays every day in June and then ends abruptly at Founders Day on July 1. The kids from grades 3 through 11 are all represented, and the entire outfield is divvied up and very colorful. Everyone wears their uniform and has their gloves ready for home-run balls. Batting practice is just ending, and Stacy finally gets to sit with Dom on the end of the front row of the bleachers. They are under the watchful eyes of Sasha and Chad, but Stacy has been nicely insistent that she needs to talk to Dom without interruption.

"You didn't go swimming?" Stacy asks Dom

"Yes, I did not go swimming," Dom says in a total smart assy sort of way.

Stacy rolls her eyes.

"My godfather taught me that joke," Dom says proudly.

"So, what happened? I saw you and Sasha in the creek?" she says.

"Sooo, I get back up to my room, and Tulpen is scratching at the window. Somebody closed it!" he starts to tell the story, "I let her in, and she jumps up on the bed and tells me to give her a big rubdown."

"She told you?" Stacy asks but kind of believes it.

"Well, not told, you know; you got a cat, right? I know what all her different meows mean," he says.

"Oh yes, I have a cat. Tabitha is her name," Stacy says with a smile.

Dom smiles back. "Yeah."

"So, I lay down next to her on the bed and started petting her, and before I knew it, it was an hour and a half later.

"You fell asleep," Stacy guesses correctly.

"I had been up late the night before with Rich," he says.

"I was helping him practice the story-time speech Chief Charley had him working on," Dom says in full story mode. He takes a swig from his orange crush. Stacy nods intently. "And we also listened to, like, seven James Brown records"

"James Brown?" Stacy asks like she knows who he is, "but why James Brown?"

Dom finishes his big swig, "Confidence, JB gives him superhero-like strength."

"Oh," Stacy says without saying the word, just making a big O with her lips.

Stacy unwraps a lollipop from her skirt pocket and licks it, then points it at Dom like a wand.

"We must be formally introduced," she switches lollipop hands and extends her right hand, "Dominix Blue, I am Stacy Long Feather Stone. I come from Lakota land like my mother. We are full-blooded Lakota, and I can see visions in our dreams."

With the word "dreams," Dom's eyes get big.

"I knew it!" Stacy wags her lollipop at Dom like a mother scolds her child.

Dom is speechless.

"I have seen you in my dreams for a whole month. When I met your brother, I knew it wasn't you even though you two are identical."

"Only in the way we look," Dom says disappointedly. "We are nothing alike."

"Not true," Stacy says and licks her lollipop some more.

Dom looks at her curiously. Stacy bites her lollipop, and half of it falls out of her mouth. It is the only ungraceful thing he has ever seen her do.

She catches the pieces and blushes just a little. She composes herself, "You both are lousy at basketball."

Dom makes an unapproving face. She smiles at him hoping he understands she is kidding.

"So, I was in your dreams?" he says, getting serious.

"One dream," she holds up the lollipop stick. "There is a cornfield, then a high rise building …" She says and then Dom jumps in.

"The clouds fly past the wrong way, then a burning bush" He pauses to remember, "Then an adult woman with purple feathers in her hair," Stacy strokes one of the feathers just as he says it.

Dom points to her.

"An adult man with a No. 37 green basketball jersey, arms folded," she says keeping the image going. They both fold their arms, looking at each other.

Stacy has the stick in her mouth waiting for Dom to continue, "There is a table with cables on the floor," he says.

Then they both say together, "A blinding light and a voice that says …." They both stop in unison pause, and then speak again together.

"Don't be afraid."

Dom turns and looks out to the game, processing what just happened.

Stacy reaches into her pocket and gets another lollipop out.

Stacy gives him a moment then scoots right up next to him. He is still staring at the field, oblivious to the game. The batter takes a walk. The whole crowd starts to chant, "Tulip" clap-clap, "Tulip," clap-clap, "Tulip"…

Dom blocks out everything but Stacy's voice.

"I had the same dream for all of June back in Lakota. I have had lots of different cool dreams, but never the same one for a month and never as clear as this one. In the last ten days of the month, you entered the dream at the same place, and you would wave your finger at me to come to you. Then you started saying one phrase, Founders Day. Our two families were moving to Mistletoe anyway, but because of you in my dream, I convinced everybody to move here on July 1."

"Founders Day," Dom says without looking at her.

"So, we moved because everybody in our families trusts my dreams. We got here, and I didn't know why we had to rush. Then I met you, but it's really Deacon. I meet Tulpen, and Mr. Lazarus is everywhere. Then Chief Charley died after he gave us a vision quest, and finally we met," she says, and with her thoughts, she asks Dom to look at her.

Dom turns, and their eyes connect.

"I think something big is going to happen with all of us—you, me, all these friends."

Dom is now deep in connected thought with Stacy.

"And it's got something to do with our dreams," he says.

There is the crack of a bat. Terry Hardson sprints to the wall in front of the front row where Stacy and Dom are talking. They don't break concentration. Terry leaps at the wall. Everyone around Dom and Stacy stand up for a home run ball. Terry climbs the wall with an outstretched glove. The ball is headed for the small space between Stacy and Dom. Terry catches the ball and his glove gently brushes the lollipop stick Stacy is holding up and barely touches Dom's shoulder. They don't even notice. The crowd gasps as one, and Terry pulls the ball back onto the field in his glove, inning over.

Dom keeps looking into Stacy's eyes and gently speaks confidently like a sweaty James Brown, "We gotta tell the others."

Stacy purses her lips, thinking of his plan and gently nods her head up and down.

8

LOLLIPOPS AND LICORICE

It is Friday at 5 o' clock. Izzy and Cecilia walk up to the base of the tree-house from Cecilia's place. They have their sleeping bags and are ready for the weekly girl's sleepover. They are in a great mood. Izzy has been mowing lawns all week. She has done four more than her triplet sisters, and as a reward, her dad gave her two days off. She started the celebration last night by getting a sleepover with Cecilia. Izaak was around most of the time, so there wasn't much girl time, but that ends tonight.

The four girls have had full reign of the treehouse for over a year now after winning the big bet over the boys. The treehouse shall host ladies night on Fridays, and the boys can have it on Saturdays. They are chatting as they walk, then hear music coming from above. It is faint and kind of scratchy. Then it stops. Then it starts back up again from earlier in the song. There is also singing. Is that Wu?

Izzy and Cecilia climb up the ladder.

Wu is in a black British bowler hat like from that James Bond movie. She is wearing black stockings, black shorts with a red stripe on the side, and a black tank top like Stacy wears. She also has a ton of makeup on her face. She is trying to dance around in lady's heels that are too big. They are probably from her mom's closet. She is playing a tape recorder, and it sounds awful.

She sings the chorus to the main song from Cabaret, just like Liza. She sees the girls, but she doesn't stop. She seems happy with the atten-tion. Izzy and Cecilia crawl up and into a corner, yielding all the space to Wu. Wu dances and trips and clunks around the treehouse in a very happy mood. They watch in disbelief. She finishes the song and tips her oversize hat, then falls to the floor. The tape keeps rolling. Wu gets a look of minor panic, then scurries over to shut it off. She looks to her friends.

They are stunned.

Before they can say a word, Wu says, "Call me Sally!" she says into a hairbrush.

Izzy smiles and beams at her best friend, "So the parents let you go see the movie *Cabaret* after all."

"Nope" Wu says confidently," I snuck out yesterday. My older brother Vladistock covered for me." Wu catches her breath. "I saw it twice, had to make sure the recording worked out."

"And did it?" Cecilia says questioning the audio quality.

Wu gives her a look but is too happy to be upset. She gets back into position and signals Cecilia to push play again. Wu takes a stance, posing. She winks at the girls and whispers, "Sally!"

The song starts and she sings along.

Wu is feeling extra uninhibited and puts on a show for her friends. It is the start of a memorable girl's poker night. They call it poker night to mess with the boys. They played poker one night but got bored with it, but they keep the deck of cards around to keep the boys guessing.

Sasha and Stacy arrive about thirty minutes later. The girls settle in for a night of catching up on all the wild events that have taken place just since last Sunday morning. Stacy joins them without any hesitation from the others. There is no hazing for the new girl. Stacy was smart and brought lots of food. She hauls up a big box using the pully system Mr. Black installed at the bottom of the crow's nest. Stacy asked her mom to make Tatonka Jerky and she brought a big bag of her favorite lollipops and all flavors of licorice. She remembered Sasha mentioning that it was the one candy all four girls liked. Big points for the memory on that one.

There is gentle chit chat about Wu's new passion and the latest saga of Sasha dealing with her older brothers. Izzy keeps quiet. Turns out she has been waiting to quiz Stacy on a few things. The mood is very happy with Cecilia keeping the tunes hopping, playing KTOE and a little album rock on KEXL FM. Sasha loves these nights where she can just be a girl.

Living in a mostly boy house tries her patience.

The sun has set and the lantern is lit. They hang it from the ceiling hook just like Mr. Black taught them so as not to be a fire hazard. There is finally a slight lull in conversation. Izzy jumps in.

"Stacy, I am curious about something," she says in an official tone.

All the girls can feel the shift in the conversation.

Stacy gets a new lollipop, puts it in her mouth, and sits back ready for the question.

"Shoot," she says.

"I am curious about these dreams that you and Dom have shared, but I am very curious about something I can't explain or understand," Izzy says and waits for a response.

Stacy plays with the lollipop and keeps eye contact with Izzy. "Yes, keep going." Stacy intensifies her eye contact to try and look deeper into Izzy's mind.

"That's it," Izzy says excitedly, I can feel something happening in my brain and in my body. I feel calmer and all happy and fuzzy at the same time. You guys feel it?" she says looking at the others.

Stacy breaks eye contact with Izzy. She looks away and focuses on Tulpen in the corner. Stacy just now realizes that the cat is in the tree-house with them.

Cecilia is the only other one to respond, "Huh?"

Izzy seems flustered, "Wait, I think it's gone now; ya'll felt that, right?"

"I kinda felt something, but it's gone now," Sasha says backing up her friend.

Izzy collects her thoughts and is waiting for the other girls to maybe say something. She sits up straight and collects just the right words.

"I have felt this fuzzy feeling only when Stacy is around and even more when she looks into my eyes." She says calmly trying to convey a serious thought. "It's like there is some sort of power coming from you," She looks right at Stacy but not accusingly, more like she is perplexed and curious.

Stacy freezes up. She spins the lollipop in her mouth like it's a distraction for her and maybe something to throw off the others. She remains quiet and only glances at Izzy and then back at Tulpen. She doesn't make direct eye contact.

Izzy sits up on her knees to more directly focus her gaze. She works up her nerve, then asks directly to Stacy.

"Are you a witch or something?"

Stacy laughs, then ponders the thought seriously like it may be a bad thing, but then laughs again but more nervously.

"I wish I was a witch; that would explain a lot!" she giggles and then realizes how personal that may have been.

She looks at the others and sees them with concerned faces and not judging looks.

She crunches her lollipop and eats it like candy. She chews and finishes it. She then sets the stick down next to her and settles in to tell a story.

"I can't explain it." Stacy chooses her words carefully. "My dad calls it a sparkly thing. He calls it a tingly, sparkly thing." She looks to Tulpen while she talks so the gaze in her eyes doesn't connect with any of the girls. Tulpen does not blink and keeps her calm.

"My mother claims that I may have inherited some Shaman, medicine woman qualities from her grandmother. All of our family from the dawn of time until now has been pure Lakotan. She is very proud of our heritage. It makes perfect sense to her that I can calm people with a touch or a connection with my eyes." I didn't realize it was something different until I found out that no one else in my family did anything like what I do."

"What do you call it?" Izzy asks very seriously.

"Awake Dreams," Stacy says firmly.

She moves her eyes away from Tulpen. She takes a deep breath, closes her eyes, and then opens them. She slowly connects with each girl one at a time, but briefly. She thinks of each one as she does this.

Stacy focuses her eyes on Cecilia.

Cecilia, very musical and knowledgeable, how do you know so many songs? Stacy thinks as she looks her way. Cecilia smiles.

She spins her gaze to Wu who is determined to learn more and more and understand why things are the way they are. As she looks at Wu, she thinks, and Wu nods yes.

Her head rotates to Sasha, she connects. *Sasha, so confident. I could really use your friendship. We can be the leader of these ladies, and the boys!*

Sasha smirks a bit.

She reconnects with Izzy and looks deep into her eyes. *Izzy, you are clever and smart. I will never be able to get anything past you.* She sends the thought through her eyes to Izzy .

"That's more than a dream" Izzy says. Izzy sits back with her back against the wall. She is right next to Tulpen and pets her calmly. She looks down at the purring cat and then divulges her thoughts.

"I have very colorful dreams. Colors everywhere. It's like they are filling up my head. My mind is like an indoor theater, and the colors are everywhere. Then Tulpen is there, and it is quiet and peaceful. I have this same dream two or three times a week. I have never told anyone about them," Izzy says. Tulpen raises up and moves over to Wu.

"Mine is in a library, colored books on all the shelves." Wu says and receives a head nudge from Tulpen.

"And Tulpen?" Izzy asks.

"On the counter by the checkout, every dream, every Wednesday night." Stacy feels an overwhelming sense of belonging, topped off with fuzzy happiness.

Tulpen walks over to Cecilia.

"All my dreams are rock concerts. I go to sleep with the transistor on and my earplugs in," Cecilia says, wishing she had a better story.

"But you have dreams, right?" Izzy asks.

"Yes," Cecilia responds. She is cradling Tulpen's head in her hands and giving her a face massage. Tulpen purrs louder and switches her tail. "The sound quality is amazing in my head!" She smiles at Wu. Tulpen moves over to Sasha who looks a little scared.

There is a pause. Sasha concentrates on petting Tulpen. She rubs her entire body from front to back four times before she speaks.

"There is color," she says softly. "Color everywhere," a single tear rolls down her cheek.

"Where is your dream?" Izzy pries gently.

Sasha continues to pet Tulpen, stroking her rhythmically.

"It's in the school gym," she says but hesitates. She looks around at the girls for support. Cecilia takes her non-petting hand. Sasha startles but accepts it. "Dom is always there with me, holding my hand."

Saturday morning
Sitting on a stage
Colors swirling around my head like wind
The sound of leaves blowing in the trees
Colors are the trees
Warmth
Sun rays of warmth
Purring
Gentle purring

Izzy wakes up but keeps her eyes closed. She realizes she just had a new dream, but she wants to be awake and still present in the dream. Where is this place? Is it in the in between places that Stacy seems to be able to visit? She listens intently. Purring, she still hears the purring. The colors slowly fade from her dream state, and now she is fully in awakened state. Eyes still closed.

She still hears the purring. She doesn't hear it in her brain anymore, but with her ears. She is fully awake with eyes closed. Can she see inside her own eyelids without opening them? She still feels warmth on her face. It was in her dream; now it is on her face. She tries to look into the backs of her eyelids. It is bright. It looks like a mixture of yellow and red. It feels like the sun is in her closed eyes.

Her head is sideways on her pillow. She remembers where she is before she opens her eyes. She is in the treehouse. She wonders if the others are still asleep. She still hears the purring.

Izzy opens her eyes. Tulpen is inches from her sun-drenched face. Tulpen is staring at her. Izzy locks eyes with her and sends her a thought.

Good morning, Tulpen, she thinks and sends it into her eyes.

About time you woke up! a thought comes to Izzy from Tulpen.

Izzy sits up with a startle. She keeps her eyes fixed on Tulpen's eyes.

Did I just communicate with a cat!? she thinks loudly.

All the others have gotten up and taken off, Tulpen thinks and then looks away. Izzy receives the thought. She looks around and sees that she and Tulpen are the only ones in the treehouse.

She reaches over and pets Tulpen's back. She gives her four long strokes of her hand from her head to her tail.

Tulpen gives that look-away cat smile that all cats love to do. Her tail swishes lively.

Izzy gets up, puts on her shoes and heads out, down the ladder. She knows where everybody is at the moment. She walks down the creek path behind Mistletoe Mansion. She crosses Woodlawn Avenue under the elevated train. She crosses the street and enters the park. She gets on the jogging path and heads down about a block to the skateboarders' concrete ditch. Rich and Izaak are sitting on the ledge of the ditch talking. Their skateboards are sitting idle by their side. Dom's brother Deacon pops up on his board. He tries to land after turning a semicircle but instead loses his board, and he runs down the ditch wall without falling.

Cecilia and Ringo are playing ukuleles on the other edge of the skate ditch across from Izaak and Rich. Behind them, Wu is sitting on the bench under a big pecan tree, reading. Izzy walks around to share her thoughts with Wu. She uses the walking bridge, crosses the ditch and sits next to her good friend. Wu is reading a new library book from Pinky's; *The Water Method Man* by John Irving. It is 11:11 in the morning. Izzy looks across the ditch to Rich and Izaak. She waves at them.

Izaak waves back.

"Hey man, have you ever noticed how Chad is always with Stacy?" Rich says to Izaak.

"Yeah," Izaak remarks without much thought.

Rich ponders if he should tell Izaak about his solo walk with Stacy and the new bike he is getting for her. He decides against it. He is staring off across the park, watching a small group of four by the basketball courts.

"Oooh, almost; try again" Izaak says to Deacon who is still trying to land a trick on his skateboard. Izaak claps encouragement.

By the basketball courts, Dom, Sasha, Chad, and Stacy are walking around on a small, purposeful mission; beer cans.

Stacy is next to a trash can and leans over. She brings up a can and shows it to Dom, "Lone Star Lite?" she asks.

"Nope, Zoltar has that one already," Dom says plainly.

The four quickly move on from the trash can by the courts. They head for the picnic tables next. Saturday mornings are good times to look for new treasures for Zoltar's beer can collection. This is the first time any girls have tagged along with Dom on this project. Usually this is a Dom and Zoltar thing. Dom is always amazed at how much beer people will drink on a Friday night.

"Hey guys, the girls and I had a good idea for tonight before ya'lls sleepover and after Rich does his story reading." Sasha says to the group while they walk.

Dom turns and gives a look to go on.

"Kick the Can!" Sasha says with hopeful returned excitement.

"Cool!" Dom says genuinely. He looks to Chad, and he nods a big yes with a smile.

"We thought that after Rich does his story, he may want to do something fun and less stressful," Sasha says.

"He seems nervous about the campfire tonight," Stacy adds.

Dom stops walking and turns to address the group. They stop as well.

"Yes," Dom chooses his words thoughtfully, "This is an important step for Rich. Some of the other elders will be there also!" Dom says with pride for his good friend Rich.

Stacy looks to Sasha.

"We also thought that it would be good to have a few more kids around to offset the adults being there," Sasha says.

Dom ponders the thought. "Good idea" he says while still processing the idea. "Then there would be more kids for Kick the Can," He says.

"That's what we thought too!" Stacy says happily agreeing with Dom.

They continue to walk toward the picnic tables. They find a treasure at the second table. Import cans from Belgium. Dom has seen these in the coolers at Pinky's. Dom finds two relatively clean ones and puts them into the bag Chad has been dutifully carrying.

"What does Zoltar do with all these cans?" Stacy asks with a bit of an icky face, seeing the dirty condition of some of the rejected collectibles.

"Well," Dom says delightfully and begins to tell a story. He holds up a Carlsburg can, "It started when we used to come here on Saturday mornings. We found two very tall thirty-two-ounce cans in perfect condition. We sat on the jogging path and scraped the tops of the cans on the concrete. Zoltar saw his cousin do this once. After scrapping enough, the top fell off and there was just the open can with a jagged edge. We then went to Mr. Blacks shed and found some sand paper. We sanded the edges of the opening until we could put our lips on it"

"Eewww," Stacy interrupts.

"We cleaned them up before that" Dom continues with a smile. You know it's a good story when you can get a good eeewww from a girl.

"So, we get the two cans all cleaned up, and then we go to Pinky's and get a couple cream sodas. We come back to the park and sit close to the ranger station by the pool where the park cops hang out. We pour our amber-colored sodas into the clean beer cans and sit back and wait." Dom pauses to see any reactions. Sasha has her arms folded. Obviously this is not the first time she has heard this story. Stacy looks intrigued. Chad's facial expressions never change that much.

"So, Zoltar and I are kicked back swigging our drinks and waiting for the park cops to stroll by. They do." Dom starts to laugh at this own story. "We got 'em good!" Dom bends over laughing.

"Zoltar tells it better," Sasha says and motions for the others to follow her to the next table. "Very poor ending," she says walking away.

Four tables later, the group comes upon an occupied table. It is a man reading his newspaper. There is a to-go coffee cup on the table in front of him. The headline of the news reads, "Ethiopia Holds Elections." The group is almost past the table when the man sets down the paper and says, "Hello, kids." It is Mr. Lazarus.

The group is startled. Sasha is first to speak. "Hello Mr. Lazarus"

"Good morning, group. It is a fine Saturday for a walk," he says delightfully and stands up. "I don't believe I have formally introduced myself to any of your group. My name is Mr. Lazarus." He puts out his hand to shake.

Chad moves in first and gives him a firm grip. Stacy follows, then Dom and Sasha. "Welcome to Mistletoe," Sasha says in her leader tone.

Mr. Lazarus sits back down. "I wanted to check in with some of you. Miss Maxwell from your block invited me to the campfire tonight to hear Mr. Mistletoe deliver his story. Is that OK with ya'll?" He hesitates on the word *ya'll* to make sure he says it right.

The kids look at each other, then settle on Sasha.

"That sounds fine," Sasha says in her official tone. "We look forward to a good night," she says, wondering slightly if that's really how adults talk.

Mr. Lazarus picks up his paper again and says, "Rich will be just great, I have full confidence in his storytelling abilities."

"He's better than Dom!" Sasha mutters to Stacy but just loud enough for Dom to hear.

Dom gives her a dirty look.

Deacon is concentrating hard on his thirty-ninth try. He sets up on the side of the ditch close to Ringo and Cecilia. He rolls down that side and up the other side by Rich and Izaak. He goes up in the air with a hand on the ledge. He holds the board with his other hand, pivots, and puts the board back to his feet and on the concrete headed back down the wall of the ditch.

"He did it," Izaak shouts. This breaks Rich's concentration. He was watching Izzy's two sisters who are looking at him on break from mowing the lawn across the street behind them. Rich reconnects with the event, and they get up to applaud. Deacon rides across the base of the ditch and has enough momentum to land next to Ringo and Cecilia. He drops his board and runs around with his arms raised high. Rich and Izaak slap hands back and forth like they have seen on American Bandstand.

"That was amazing" "Do It again" Izzy's two other triplet sisters are now standing right behind Rich, startling him. "What?" Rich says, turning to see them up close.

"That was amazing," "Do it again," one speaks, then the other finishes.

Roxilita DaVinci is the redhead and Anjolina DaVinci is the jet black, raven-haired sister. Izzy is the blonde.

"I, uh, don't think he can. It took him all morning to do one!" Rich says talking directly to the girls who are giving him their full attention.

"You do it," "Yeah, you try," They say one after the other.

"Uhh," Rich stammers a bit

Izaak turns around and says, "Rich is still a knee rider"

"A knee rider?" "What's that?" the girls talk in stereo, left speaker to right speaker.

Izaak grabs his board, puts his knees on the board, and uses his hands to push himself along. He points himself in Deacon's direction.

"Oh," the girls say together.

"Tell them about tonight—Kick the Can!" Izaak hollers back at him.

The girls both look at Rich. They both take sips from their bottles of Dr. Pepper at the same time.

"Uh yeah, we're all playin Kick the Can tonight on the block, like 9:30 p.m. Ya'll come on out"

"Sounds" "Great" they say one after the other.

Wu finishes a chapter and places a bookmark after chapter eight. She sets the book down, stands, and stretches. Izzy has been waiting patiently for this break. She waits for Wu to finish her stretch. It reminds her of when Tulpen stretches. Don't ever pet a cat in mid-stretch. Wu finishes and sits back down next to Izzy on the bench. Izzy has an excited look on her face. Wu has seen this before. She knows that Izzy is dying to tell her something.

"Yes?" Wu says with smug curiosity.

"Are you sitting down?" Izzy asks.

Wu looks at herself, then gives Izzy a stupid look.

"I can communicate with cats!"

10

SUNSET

Dom and Sasha decide to sit in the back of the storytelling gathering around the firepit. They sit on a bench where Rich can focus on them if he gets nervous while telling the story. He has written it all down. He knows, however, that all good storytellers do not read from pages. They tell the story from memory and from the spirit within them. "Kind of like a sermon," Izzy tells Rich. That analogy actually didn't work too well. It only made Rich more nervous. He has been gaining confidence in his storytelling abilities by listening to his James Brown records. He doesn't want to come off as flashy as JB, but he gains strength from his musical vibe and his stage presence.

On top of all the worry, Rich is dealing with the fact the he is the first non-Lakotan to ever be asked to tell the oral history of the Mistletoe Founders. It kind of makes sense when you think about it, though. His great-grandfather was the founder of the town that was envisioned by the Lakotans as the ideal community back at the turn of the century. Richard Mistletoe I came to the Lakotan elders with an idea. None of his Mistletoe bloodline ancestors since Richard I have had anything to do with the Lakotan ideal of the town. Rather, they only saw the growth of the Mistletoe Delivery Service and the money potential. MDS is an international company, and it all started here in this ideal town setting. Richard I was the only Mistletoe brother, who had the compassion of the Lakota people at heart. Chief Charley must have known it was time when he gave Rich IV the honor.

Sunset is coming, and people are arriving for this first test run of the story. Chief Charley's rocking chair remains empty. A gentle breeze moves it slightly when his name is invoked. The crowd of adults and youth gather near the chair at the firepit on Pinky's storefront deck. Grandma Maxwell, who is an elder, has brought along Alex Standing Foot, Bluford's dad, as the other elder representative. Mr. Lazarus has come along also. Steve Hamilton is here with his grandmother. This is the first time anyone from the block has seen her away from her house. Rich has mentioned that our group really needs a distinctive name. "Kids from the Block" just doesn't sound like anything special.

Cecilia invited Ringo, and she brought an extra guitar along to give to Cecilia. They were asked to play background music to set the tone. They have been practicing and learning since VBS. Rich invited Izzy's two sisters to come early before Kick the Can. There is something special about Roxi and Anjo. They look just like Izzy except for the hair, but he enjoys looking at them. They bring him a sense of calm.

Sasha invited Jaydici, her Rhino Girls basketball friend from church to tag along. Sasha's two older brothers come dressed in ceremonial costumes. They are part of the Hispanic Lakota delegation. The Mexican people supported the Lakota movement after the Civil War and have shared a long standing peace. The Quinterro family has roots in the original Founding of Mistletoe as trusted allies. Wu decided to bring her brother as a thank you for the other night. Vladistok is one of her adopted brothers. He is still learning English as his second language to Russian. A few eyebrows were raised when Mr. Lazarus conversed with him at their greeting in Vlad's native tongue.

The crowd is assembled, and the fire is crackling with not too much vigor but not too wimpy either. Chad took it upon himself to be the pyro tonight. Stacy is wearing new feathers woven into her hair. She has a mini-beaded vest over her usual black tank top and pleated black and grey skirt. Stacy's mom is sitting next to her, cross-legged on the deck. She does not look much older than her daughter. Chad's dad is sitting in a chair in the back next to Mr. Lazarus. They are chit chatting about London. Rich stands up. This signals that the story is about to begin.

Rich has a collection of papers in his hand. They are handwritten and have many notes scribbled next to neat handwriting. He looks at them carefully. He looks at Grandma Maxwell and Alex Standing Foot. They remain stoic and respectful. Rich leans in over the fire and places the paperwork into the highest jumping flame. They quickly catch fire and turn to ash. A gentle blue smoke rises up and takes the gathering's attention.

Rich places his hands behind his back and speaks softly, "This is the story of Chief Brown Stag and his brother Richard the First. It is not the story of Falling Rock." The adults laugh out loud. Rich smiles. He has broken the ice with a good-natured historically correct joke that he can refer to later. All of his anxiety about this project has fallen away, and he can now tell the story from his Spirit Heart.

The whole of the story lasts about forty minutes. Rich stumbles with some details here and there, but for a first timer at his young age, all are impressed. Alex Standing Foot is first to praise his talents. He invites him to come to informal meetings with other elders to train and better learn the story. Grandma Maxwell is beaming with pride. It is now time for some fun. Most of the gathered group head back to the block for a game of Mistletoe Kick the Can.

Dom and Sasha gather all the players by the Monument Archway in front of Grandma Maxwell's house. It serves as one of the home-base lookout spots for the hide-and-seek portion of the game. You can climb onto the monument and get up to second-story level, but it is not as high as the crow's nest at the opposite end of the block. The treehouse with its higher vantage point is the preferred base and lookout spot. Dom and Sasha are ready to explain the game, Mistletoe style, but first they must have equal numbers on each team. It is an unwritten rule that Kick the Can is always boys versus girls.

The boys team shapes up nicely. Dom, Rich, and Izaak are veterans of this version. Chad joins Sasha's brothers who are older and have passed the game along to the younger block kids. They really need a better name. Steve Hamilton has joined them. What a nice surprise that he has played kick ball and is joining in with the group here also. Wu's brother Vlad is two years older but oblivious to the ways of his new country. He agrees to play, and Izaak gives Wu the nod that he will watch out for him. Deacon Blue and Luke Stone decide not to play, so that opens up a spot for young

Jordan Simms. His and Chad's dad, Chile Simms, agrees to help round out the numbers by joining. He agrees to be a lookout.

The girls counter with a very formidable team. Sasha, Wu, Izzy, Stacy, and Cecilia are joined by Anjo, Roxi, Ringo, and Jaydici. Stacy's mom agrees to be lookout for the girls, amounting to four veterans and six newcomers.

The street lights have been on for quite a while. This is usually when the games begin, but Rich's fire-time story was a very welcome preamble. All are now gathered. Many other adults are on porches tonight, curious to watch the game. Many new faces have invigorated the veteran players. All porch lights are asked to be turned off. Grandma Maxwell is hosting Mr. Lazarus at this end near the Monument Archway.

"First thing we need to do ..." Dom begins then looks to Sasha.

"Decide home base and lookout spots," Sasha finishes and smiles at Dom.

"And boundaries," Izaak blurts out.

"Getting to that, doofus," Cecilia pinches her brother's arm.

"Yes, boundaries, but first we must select obstacle course runners to see which team gets choice of lookout spots." Dom states while leading the rules portion.

"The obstacle course requires agility and grace and strength," Sasha adds.

"OK, now, The two teams go huddle up and decide on runners. Boys will be the Gray Team, and girls will be Green." Dom directs.

Sasha's brother, Raul Quinterro, will run for the boys. At fourteen, he is the middle child of the family.

Jaydici is only ten, like most of the kids, but she is picked for her speed and agility.

"We have a new obstacle course this time thanks to the new members of the block." Sasha continues up front. "The Hamilton house is in bounds now as well"

"Thank you to the Simms, Hamilton, and Stone families," Dom adds.

"What's the course?" Izaak asks impatiently.

"Start here at the archway, run across the bridge into the elementary playground. Go through the dome monkey bars. Collect the Green or

Gray bandana from the playground castle. Run back across the bridge. Hop the Hamilton's fence, hop into the Stone's yard without getting licked by either dog. Retrieve a dog toy, hop back over, cross the street to the even side, circle behind Simms's house and come back by the Blue's house. Go through the garden hose spider web without touching the hose. If you touch, the sprinklers will activate. Then go to the Mistletoe Mansion gazebo and find the second bandana. Come back to the archway first and your team picks the lookout spot. Simple," Sasha finishes and sticks her tongue out at Izaak.

Sasha produces a whistle on a chord from inside her shirt. She looks at the two runners and tweets.

Jaydici and Raul take off running. Raul makes it to the bridge first but just barely. Raul gets to the dome monkey bars and goes head first through a big hole near the bottom. Jaydici jumps and grabs on with her feet already through a hole, and she clears the bars into the inside. She then lands quickly, jumps through another hole, and rolls a perfect tumble on the ground and is up again ahead of Raul. Raul struggles to get back out.

Jaydici climbs up on the castle playground by the slide. She finds the green bandana and is back on the ground running before Raul can get totally out of the dome monkey bars. It's not even close after that. Jaydici hops fences and whistles at the dogs. They sit and stay. She speeds around the house and clears the spider web hoses with another perfect tumble. She catches her breath, walking back from the gazebo to the archway as Raul gives up at the Hamilton's fence. She hands the bandanas/flags to Sasha, turns to Dom, and puts a hand on her side, saying, "Crow's nest." Dom sends Jordan to get the boys' other bandana from the gazebo.

Dom and Sasha finish up with the rules and boundaries:

the boundaries are easy. Follow the creek from behind Mr. Fremont's house where it goes under Lake street and follow the "L" shape behind all the houses to the bend and then behind the treehouse all the way to Woodlawn Avenue sidewalk. The other "L" shape goes from that corner behind the mansion and Woodlawn back behind all the other houses to the diner at the corner of Lake and Woodlawn. Then follow the bend up Lake street to the creek behind Mr. Fremont's. Only the insides of houses are off limits, unless you gotta go pee. Any other structures are fair game. Nobody has had enough guts to hide in Mr. Fremont's pool shed in his backyard, but you never know.

The game itself is easy as well. Most everybody hides but the guards, lookouts, and the seekers. Seekers try to find the other team's hiders. Hiders hide or look for the flag. Jail guards hide the flags. When you find a hider, you collect their long tube sock, and they go to the other team's base that serves as jail. Each player has a long tube sock stuck halfway out the back of the shorts. Each team has a jail guard who tries to catch people by snagging the sock.

Those who run to Kick the Can release their team from jail if they Kick the Can without getting caught. The can is an old paint can with rocks in it. Lookouts and seekers have walkie talkies to communicate. If after forty minutes, not everyone has been found, each hidden player gets fifty points for their team. Each caught runner is ten points for the opposing team. One hundred points are awarded when you find each of the two hidden flags or bandanas. The team with the most points after forty minutes wins, and everyone is called in with Sasha's whistle.

Izaak and Izzy are selected as guards. They have ten minutes to hide the flags. Everybody else has to sit on the monument bench facing away from the block and playing field. Mrs. Stone and Mr. Simms serve as lookouts. Rich and Cecilia are picked as seekers.

The first game begins.

Chad walks toward Sasha's house. He goes around the back and walks the creek. He comes back up between his house and Mr. Fremont's. There is a dark spot on top of his fence by the front side of his house. He crawls up and simply stands on top of the five-foot-high fence. He remains still as a board next to the house. He is oblivious to the boys yelling and Izzy's sisters squealing for the next forty minutes. From this spot, he can watch Grandma Maxwell and Mr. Lazarus sitting on her porch. She has a flashlight and every now and then shines a light on where she thinks a boy might be hiding. This is not official cheating behavior since she is not officially "playing." Luke and Deacon try the same tactic from Luke's bedroom window, but their flashlight is lame compared to Grandma Maxwell's. Mostly Mr. Lazarus is talking with Grandma. Chad can't hear what they are saying, but he can catch his tone enough to know that Mr. Lazarus is very curious.

Chad's spot is very quiet otherwise. About twenty-five minutes into the first round, he hears a chair being scooched on Mr. Fremont's upstairs front porch. From his hiding spot on top of the fence, he can see the orange glow of his cigarette.

The whistle blows signaling the end of the first round. Chad hops down into his side yard so as not to give up his good hiding spot. He wanders back to the archway base to big applause from the boy's Gray team. He was the only player not found, and his fifty points puts the boys over the top. Mrs. Simms breaks out a box full of nutty buddy ice cream cones from the family freezer before the second round begins. Chad looks up and sees Mr. Fremont smoking away with that eerie orange glow. All the lights in his house are turned off as if he were included in the game.

Round two begins, and this time Chad walks down Lake street and behind Mr. Fremont's house. He circles behind and comes back into his own yard. He comes back to the same spot as round one but with a twist. There are a stack of big boxes from the move that MDS hasn't taken away yet. Chad climbs into an upside-down refrigerator box. He can stand inside of it. He pokes eye holes into the sides. He can survey all sides and be ready to run if found. Or is that against the rules? He can't remember.

Eight and a half minutes into round two, Chad notices Tulpen is slowly moving from in front of his house toward the archway. He wonders if anyone was assigned to watch over her tonight. The urgency has died down since earlier in the busy week. She walks slowly but surely until she crouches down at a sudden sound. Wu is running for the can. She kicks it and yells, "Green Team Free!" She runs right past Tulpen and into Dom's back yard. Chad keeps his eyes fixed on the rainbow colored cat.

Tulpen sits for a bit and watches for any more sudden movements. Chad looks over and sees Mr. Lazarus is now standing and leaning on Grandma Maxwells railing. He is watching Tulpen also. Chad hears movement on Mr. Fremont's upstairs porch. The orange glow goes sailing off the porch, flicked from his hands. There is a gun. Chad throws the box off and heads for Tulpen. She turns to look at Chad coming at her. Chad dives just as the pop of a high powered pellet gun goes off.

Chad feels a bite in his upper back left shoulder. Tulpen quickly turns around and runs toward the treehouse. Chad lands on the ground, and now the bite feels warm. He reaches back and senses an oozing of blood. Mr. Lazarus is next to him and has a handkerchief on his wound and pressing hard. He rolls Chad over, and Grandma Maxwell is hovering over him. Mr. Lazarus heads toward the treehouse and runs into Izaak who is headed for the can. Just as he is about to kick, the whistle blows. Mr. Lazarus stops his forward progression and catches both shoulders in his hands.

"Tulpen! Go find her. She was headed for the treehouse," Mr. Lazarus says franticly.

Without any hesitation, Izaak heads after Tulpen. Izaak sees her jump onto the tree and up the ladder to safety. Izaak follows cautiously but quickly.

Mr. Lazarus turns his attention back to Chad.

"He's OK," Grandma Maxwell says. "It's not too bad, go get him!"

Mr. Lazarus runs up to Mr. Fremont's front door and goes right in.

Mrs. Stone comes down from the archway lookout spot and tends to Chad. The rest of the kids start to gather. Some are complaining about the early whistle; others are just curious as to what's going on. Grandma Maxwell gathers the kids to her house, all except Stacy who goes to Chad. Mrs. Stone can feel the pellet about a quarter inch into Chad's shoulder. Mr. Simms joins them, and they head to the train to run to the hospital to get Chad fixed up.

Grandma Maxwell brings everyone else into her house and gets everybody settled until Mr. Lazarus comes back. She tells everyone what happened.

Mr. Lazarus knocks on the door about thirty minutes later. He addresses everybody.

"It's all clear kids. I think it best if we all head home tonight. I know the boys usually have the treehouse for a sleepovers, but maybe we postpone that," he says calmly.

"How is Tulpen? Dom asks.

"Tulpen is fine. Izaak has her in the treehouse. I am sure you can go see her. She is safe."

"Where is Mr. Fremont?" Izaak asks.

"He is with the police," Mr. Lazarus says matter of factly. "No more worries from him tonight."

More questions start to come, but Mr. Lazarus holds up his hands.

"Everything is safe, and it's time to get home" he says, "Your parents are here ready to take ya'll back to your respective houses. Good night, everybody, and thank you, Grandma Maxwell."

An hour and a half later, at precisely midnight, Tulpen sends all nine kids a dream.

Wind blows the big treehouse leaves;
It is sunny and warm
Tulpen is laying on the picnic table at the base of the treehouse.
She is purring and smiling that smirky cat smile.
She sends a thought
Noon.
She raises up to stretch her full body;
Wings come out of her back and extend to full expanse.
She lifts up to fly;
She lifts straight up
Up above the treehouse crow's nest.
She turns and flies over and away.
Noon, the wind whispers

11

DESTINY

All nine kids from the block, Sasha, Dom, Stacy, Chad, Cecilia, Izaak, Izzy, Wu, and Rich, have gathered at the picnic table in front of the sycamore treehouse. Only Zoltar is still missing.

It is early—11:55 a.m. Cecilia has the transistor radio on low. Big Willy has continued through his show and has stayed on the air, playing many new and wonderous songs Cecilia has never heard before. Chad has a big bandage on his back, at his left shoulder. Dom insists on showing it off to everyone. He is very happy with Chad for saving his cat. For the first time, Sasha notices that the boys and girls are mixed together. They are not in separate groups at the table. She is not sure why she notices this, but the table is filled with laughter and concern and curiosity.

Mr. Lazarus walks up, having come from the school. He crosses the bridge and stops. It appears he is counting to see that all are present. He gently nods his head to himself, pleased that all the kids are on time. They all quiet down and give him full attention. He has a box that looks very old, like a small pirate chest from a movie. He stands at the head of the table and looks at his watch. It's 11:58 a.m.

"Miss Black, make sure your radio is heard at precisely noon?" he says.

She nods and turns it up a bit. She keeps her finger ready to go louder when called for.

"I believe I have officially met each of you at some point or other in the last few days." He checks his watch again—11:59 a.m.

"I am Mr. Lazarus from, uh, Boston. Yes, Boston seems nice," he says not entirely sure of where he is from.

"I am here to give this group a name, finally. Kids? Block? These words don't quite do justice to the amazing collection of talent and young maturity before us." With that he stops and looks around the table and ends with his eyes fixed on Cecilia. He nods.

Cecilia turns up the radio to hear Big Willy coming out of a commercial,

A special request at high noon on this gorgeous summer Sunday afternoon. Yes, the clock has just ticked past the hour mark. This song comes to us from our newest fifth-grade teacher, Mr. Lazarus. Just released a week ago, it slipped under Big Willy's radar. A band from Boston, they call themselves Aerosmith. This song goes out to the Dream Prophets.

The song begins with a guitar intro then the words begin.

They listen closely to the words through the whole of the song. They seem pleased with it. Cecilia turns the radio back down and focuses back on Mr. Lazarus.

"Dream Prophets! Yes?" He says looking for approval.

All nine nod and show approval.

"Cool song," Cecilia echoes.

"That was a lovely coincidence. Tulpen alerted my attention to that tune. I picked up the single in Boston, just before traveling to Mistletoe. I thought it might be appropriate for this group. Time will tell. I know how much music means to the youth of today." Mr. Lazarus seems to be in full teaching mode, and his audience is respectful but a bit dumbfounded. Izzy raises her hand.

"Oh that's not necessary here! Yes, Miss DaVinci, a question?"

"Why has the dream gathered us all here?" she asks what the whole group is wondering.

"Oh yes, back on track, very studious," Mr. Lazarus puts his hands on the box.

"I have in this box, symbols, and trinkets of your *Destiny*" He pauses on the word *Destiny* to let it sink in.

"Twelve of you have been chosen for a lifelong task, if you choose to accept it," he says and pauses again.

"Twelve?" Sasha asks, "but there are only nine of us here."

"Zoltar will be back soon, and well, the other two will be moving here soon enough. This project is actually taking place sooner than originally planned. A number of years early, actually, but forces beyond our control have hastened the revealing of your destiny at this point in time."

Rich is smiling with the mention of Zoltar.

"Our?" Izzy asks without her hand raised, "Who is our?"

"Very good, Miss DaVinci, you are the cleverest aren't you!" He smiles with knowledge that has not yet been made clear to the group.

"Tulpen and I," he says plainly.

"How is Tulpen? I woke up this morning and she was gone," Dom asks excitedly.

"You saw her! In the dream, she flew off!" he teaches.

"She can really fly?" Izaak asks skeptically.

Mr. Lazarus smiles at the group again with knowledge, "All of your dreams from now on will only show or foretell the truth."

Another pause from the group as they ponder that thought.

"Where did she fly to?" Dom asks.

"She has business elsewhere," he says, then adds "Kittens. She has a special place she visits when she is in the feline way," he says with a sarcastic smirk.

"Kittens!" Wu says excited.

"She will be back" He says and thumps the box in front of him, bringing attention back to the task at hand.

"As you know from last night's dream, you are blessed with a new and special gift," he continues. "Your dreams are *very* important" Not just for each other but for all of humanity."

"Get out!" Izaak says out loud what he was thinking. "Sorry" he says sheepishly.

"No, I understand; this is a lot to take in. It will take time to fully understand what it means to be a Dream Prophet." Mr. Lazarus has their total attention.

"This is a lifelong commitment." He scans each set of eyes to assure that they heard him.

"Lifelong," he says again to pondering faces.

"This is also a choice. You will have time to decide if you are up to the task," he drums his fingers on the box. He pauses longer this time to let his statements sink deeper into their thoughts.

"Why are we Dream Prophets?" Izzy asks

"All will be revealed in time," Mr. Lazarus states and then waits for other possible questions.

They look around to each other but keep quiet for now.

"Are you still with me?"

They all nod seriously and cautiously. Wu is the last to acknowledge in the positive.

"Very good," Mr. Lazarus says slowly. "Here are the terms.

As I said, this is a lifelong commitment. The decision becomes final at your eighteenth birthdays. After that, there is absolutely no turning back. You will be a Dream Prophet for life."

"A Dream Prophet has specific skills that help and serve all people, and it is with this dedication that you will be working for Jesus himself," he states and pauses again

"Jesus? Like Bible Jesus?" Wu asks.

"Yes, the very one," Mr. Lazarus says matter of factly.

"But I am not sure yet if I want to be a Christian or a part of any religion," Wu says slowly and respectfully.

"Not a problem," Mr. Lazarus states and looks to Izaak.

He looks into Izaak's eyes, "Muslim, Hindu, Judaism, any faith is fine for we are all children of God." Mr. Lazarus says in his most reassuring voice.

"And again, your final decision will not come for eight more years— plenty of time to think and discern and question your dedication to the task of being a Dream Prophet."

They are stunned and quiet.

"You will have your first big decision in a few months. At the start of your fifth-grade year, you will be asked to move forward or to stop. Moving forward simply allows your skills to continue to grow. If you stop, your dreams and thoughts go back to the way they were before this week," Mr. Lazarus continues. He is reading from a small book that didn't seem to be there a minute ago.

"You can decide to go forward at any point, but just after Labor Day is your first decision. To move forward all you have to do is put your hands together in prayer and say, 'Jesus, I accept your quest.'"

Dom puts his hands together and starts to speak.

Mr. Lazarus speaks and cuts him off. "Once you decide, you will receive the first mark."

"A mark?" Dom asks with hands folded ready to pray.

"It's like a tattoo. It will appear just inside your hairline on the back of your neck. You can only show it off if you shave the hair back there." He pauses, then gets giddy, "Best thing about being a Dream Prophet is you never go bald!"

Blank faces.

"This will be more important to you, ya'll, later in life," he says realizing some of this information may not be pertinent now.

Dom starts to pray out loud, "Jesus I accept your quest."

Rich and Izaak rush over to look at the back of his neck.

Mr. Lazarus looks up to the heavens, "Just like Peter!" He remarks to his friend.

Dom sits up straight, letting Izaak move the hair on the back of his neck looking for a mark. He stops.

"Right onnn" Izaak says out loud. Izzy gives him a disappointing look. She mouths the words, "Right on," to Wu, and Wu giggles.

"Check it out" Izaak keeps his fingers spread to reveal a cross with a lightning bolt coming out of the bottom of it. Rich leans in to see it and says, "Groooovy Maaaan."

With that, all the others gather around to see what it looks like. Mr. Lazarus waits patiently for the ten-year-olds to act more like their age than the mature young people seated in front of him a minute ago.

"Hey, Izzy, you still got that Polaroid camera in your bag?" Dom asks impatiently.

"Oh, hey," she looks around in her bag. "There it is," Izzy says happily.

Izzy walks over to Dom's head. Izaak moves the hair around to get a good image. Izzy gets in close. She pushes the button, and it makes that cool whirring, buzzy sound. The picture pops out. Izzy gives it to Dom, and he stares at it until he image comes clear.

"Jesus, I accept your quest," Stacy says very calmly and seriously, with her eyes closed. She turns and opens her eyes to the rest of the group. She takes a ribbon from her skirt pocket and ties her hair up into a ponytail. Izzy comes over and gets another picture.

After a few minutes, the frenzy dies down, and Mr. Lazarus brings them back in to reveal mode once again.

"Another term of being a Dream Prophet ..." he states very teacher like.

"None of you can ever tell anybody else about being a Dream Prophet." He says very seriously. "No one can know." He looks into each of their eyes sharing the thought, *If you need to talk, you can always share thoughts with each other. I believe some of you have experienced this with each other.* He looks at each of the girls.

"What are you talking about?" Dom says and looks at a grinning Sasha.

"Go ahead Miss Quinterro, try it on Mr. Blue," Mr. Lazarus smiles fiendishly.

Dom swivels his head away from Mr. Lazarus and back at Sasha. He locks eyes with Sasha. She conjures up a thought and sends it to Dom.

"I am not a dork!" Dom says and then immediately realizes why Sasha is grinning at him with such a smug look on her face. He turns and locks eyes with Cecilia, "*I said, I am not a dork; oh my gosh, I can read minds.*"

All the girls laugh and start trying to make eye contact with the boys.

"Gentlemen, you are not reading minds; you are sharing thoughts. Continue."

The boys practice receiving thoughts from the girls and then switch it up and share with each other. This goes on happily for ten minutes or so. Mr. Lazarus is showing great patience, like he may have done this before.

They settle down and focus back on Mr. Lazarus.

"If you tell anyone about any aspect of being a Dream Prophet, you will lose your voice," Mr. Lazarus states. "You can always share with each other and have no reason to tell anyone else. This is a non-negotiable part of the deal."

Dom looks at the picture of the tattoo and exclaims, "hey my picture is gone"

He looks at Mr. Lazarus and he just smirks.

He pauses to feel the vibe of the crowd. They seem happy but stunned.

"Are we ready to open the box?" Mr. Lazarus asks.

Nods all around.

"Each of you is a Dream Prophet and that means each of you has a special gift that has started to show itself, and it will grow and enrich your life as you grow and live. I have something for each of you that will help you with your identity destiny. For this project to work, all twelve of you will have valuable gifts to give. You are a team. Every part of the team needs every other part of the team to accomplish our quest. Tulpen and I are your spirit guides, and you are the Dream Prophets. I know I am repeating myself, but this is important information." Mr. Lazarus is able to be serious and relaxed at the same time. Izzy notes to herself that the fuzzy warm feeling she feels around Stacy is very present with Mr. Lazarus also.

Mr. Lazarus opens the box by unlatching the different locks and slide bars. "Miss Cecilia, will you please take notes in your spiral notebook?"

Cecilia acknowledges.

"We will start here with Izaak and go around the table. Remember, no one person's gift is more important than another's; all gifts make this work."

Mr. Lazarus reaches into the box and pulls out a key chain. There is a medallion on the chain with a ring for keys. The medallion has the crescent moon and star logo on it. "Mr. Izaak Black, you are the engineer, designer, and transportation expert for the Dream Prophets. If something needs building, we start with you. If the group needs to go somewhere, you will provide means to travel. If the treehouse needs fixing …" He looks up at the treehouse, "you are the guy." He hands the key chain to Izaak. "This particular totem belonged to a historical figure. All the totems have, shall we say, history that pertains to each of your heritages. That information will be revealed later. Just, make sure you take care of each of these items." Mr. Lazarus watches Izaak look at the keychain very carefully. He recognizes the medallion to be the symbol for Islam.

"Miss Izabella DaVinci, here is a compass. You will be a world traveler, a photographer, and a reporter. But mostly you will need to study archeology." Izzy's eyes get big at all the information. "Miss DaVinci, do you like hats?"

"Sure, I like to wear the occasional hat" she states in a very formal way. "A fedora may be in your future!" Mr. Lazarus says with a bit of glee.

"Richard Mistletoe the fourth, you are the, treasurer, historian, and keeper of heritage. It is no coincidence that all of you have landed here in this place. This is the destination for the other two Prophets who will arrive shortly. You will be the caretaker after Mr. Black passes all of his knowledge onto you. Indeed, with last night's campfire, you have already begun your training." Mr. Lazarus stops and reaches into the box "Here is Chief Charley's zippo lighter. It's not as old as some of the totems in the box, but it has strong meaning for you," He hands it to Rich.

"Thank you," Rich says respectfully. He cradles the object in his hand like an egg.

Mr. Lazarus turns to Cecilia, "Cecilia Black, do you watch *Star Trek*? The TV show?"

"Sometimes," she looks at her brother, "with Izaak and Rich after school."

"Do you know who Lt. Uhuru is?" Mr. Lazarus asks.

"Oh yeah, she's the only reason I watch the show! Science Fiction isn't really my thing," she says and wonders why this is important to her destiny.

Mr. Lazarus hands her an old harmonica. "You will be the voice of this group and the voice of Mistletoe. Pursue your music as a way to communicate with the world. Work on your DJ skills and learn from Big Willy and the other KTOE people. Keep taking notes as you are also the secretary at meetings until you tire of it down the road. Keep practicing your guitar with Ringo. There may be a band in your future!"

Cecilia is very happy. She looks down at the harmonica and sees the name Martin is scratched into it.

"Chad Grey Fox Simms!" Mr. Lazarus looks to the end of the table. Chad has been sitting on a wooden crate at the end of the picnic table. He starts to stand up.

"Oh no, that's not needed; please sit." Mr. Lazarus motions for him to relax. "Thank you for the respect, you no doubt have been taught well by your family. You, sir, will be the group's protector and soldier. No harm shall come to this group with you on watch. Learn the ways of self-defense and nonviolent safety. Consider yourself the Bruce Lee of the Prophets. Your main concern is caring for Stacy, which of course you already are aware of. For you, I have a very old Texas Rangers badge from the late 1800s." Chad stands up again to receive the gift.

"Stacy Long Feather Stone, are you familiar with the words, Wicasa Wakan?" Mr. Lazarus says in his most serious tone.

Stacy looks paralyzed at the sound of the words. She turns slowly to meet Mr. Lazarus's eyes and whispers, "Yes, of course. It is a Lakotan honor."

"You are the group's spiritual healer and dream communicator." Mr. Lazarus reaches in and draws out a silver and turquoise locket necklace. All dreams will start with you and then be sent out to the others for now. The locket is sealed until all twelve are gathered; then more information will follow. You are also to be protected just as we protect Tulpen. You have a seed within you that is very important."

Stacy nods knowingly.

"Wu Punabi, you are a seeker!" Mr. Lazarus says with a very reassuring smile. "Do you paint?"

"Sometimes, but I keep that very private," Wu says with a shudder. "That is fine, no need to share with the world, but pursue your painting as an expression of your inner self. It will help bring you strength as you will one day lead another group outside of the Prophets." She smiles now with relief that a secret has been exposed but not trashed. "Keep reading books as your passion. You will be the librarian of the Prophets. Knowledge is your destiny. You will also bring comfort as one who listens. Keep searching and seeking for answers to all the world's questions. Here is a key to a safe deposit box that holds the oldest book in the world. There will come a time when you need to read it. Keep studying!"

Wu accepts the key very happily.

"Oh, yes, and the dancing is divine but not part of your destiny!" Mr. Lazarus winks at her.

"Sasha Looks Twice Quinterro" Mr. Lazarus addresses her with his eyes. She has her hands folded and eyes closed.

"Jesus, I accept your quest," she says calmly and opens her eyes to Mr. Lazarus.

"Miss Sasha, your destiny is as a teacher." He hands her an eagle feather. "You shall one day fashion this into a writing tool. You will also have other roles within the Prophets. We want you to train with Chad to be a protector. We also want you to learn of archeology to help Izzy. Mostly, however, you will be the leader of the Dream Prophets."

"Dominix Blue," Dom sits up and turns attention away from the cool eagle feather Sasha received.

Mr. Lazarus pulls out a pukka shell necklace from Hawaii. There is a small black figure on the necklace of a hunched figure playing a flute.

"Kokopelli!" Mr. Lazarus says "Learn what it means. You will be friend to all, and you will have no enemies.

Dom hands the necklace to Sasha and she puts it on around his neck. She lightly touches the tattoo on his neck.

"I know you will have many questions. Talk with each other and have Cecilia write them all down and keep them safe. You have a week until all of you go to camp for a week, and then another week of camp after that?" Mr. Lazarus looks to Sasha.

"Yes, we all go to Camp Flutterby and then we go to my camp: Camp Lone Hill," she says proudly

Stacy and Chad look at each other.

"I don't think your folks have told you yet," Sasha says and wonders why she already has this knowledge.

"Great, use the time to think and ponder and celebrate and worry. You are very young but also very wise and smart. Zoltar will be back soon, and you can fill him in when he gets back. I may see you around town, but Stacy can get me anytime you need me in an emergency. She can contact any of you by thought. We are connected, and we are safe. Mr. Fremont cannot harm us now."

"Where is he?" Chad asks

"He is gone," Mr. Lazarus says very abruptly.

There is an uncomfortable pause.

"OK, Dream Prophets, we have some time to think about all of this, how about some lunch on my back porch!" Sasha says taking leadership of the group.

12

AUGUST

The minivans pull into the parking lot of Redeemer Lutheran. The nine current Dream Prophets have been together at two different camps: the American Lutheran Camp in Kerville, and the LCMS conservative camp in La Grange. Izzy kept the counselors on their toes with all sorts of theological questions. Cecilia and Wu took copious amounts of notes on all their answers and almost daily notes of most of the other Prophets who had Dream questions. Cecilia filled one spiral and half of another. They become tired and ready for some alone time. Stacy reached out a couple times to Mr. Lazarus. She has set up a Sunday noon meeting. It is Friday afternoon now, and parents are at the church, ready to help kids with their bags onto the train platform and a quick ride home.

Sasha and Dom are on their own. Other parents have been charged to pick them up. As they get to the bottom of the platform stairs, they notice something. Steve Hamilton is next door to the train stop, and he is waving at them wildly. He is sitting at an outside table at the run-down Dairy Princess Ice Cream Palace. He is eating an ice cream cone with his grandma. She is quietly staring at them like she does most times from her chair on the front porch of her house. They catch Steve's eye, and now he is waving with both hands and spraying drops of ice cream on Grandma. She is unmoved. They set down their gear and walk over.

"Hey Steve, what's with all the hand gestures!" Sasha asks him.

Steve tries to act cool now and takes a lick of his cone to even out all the parts of the cone that had been disturbed by his waving. "Hey," he says.

Dom speaks up, "You looked like a chicken flapping your wings just now, what's up?"

Sasha jumps in quick, "Yeah, it looked important."

She lets Steve regain his cool. Grandma has the same look on her face. Her non-ice cream hand is in her lap, guarding her purse.

"We have new neighbors," He says very matter of fact. He knows this will interest the two kids.

"Where?" Dom asks excitedly.

"A long-haired girl moved in with Miss Maxwell on the corner. I only saw her from a distance. She's got long, black hair in braids"

"Thanks, Steve!" Sasha says and starts to grab Dom's arm to head back to the train.

"There's more," Steve says and takes a big lick of his ice cream.

Sasha and Dom turn back around.

"A big family moved into Mr. Fremont's house. Three kids, all about the same size, but one is skinny. They all have buzz cuts. I think they are triplets," he says.

"Thanks again, Steve," Dom says loudly and reaches out to shake his hand like an adult would.

Steve takes his hand and then holds it. "Think we could play kickball again soon? That was fun."

Dom looks to Sasha, "Yeah, maybe tomorrow after we all get some rest," Sasha says happily. "We've been gone for two weeks at camp." She takes Dom's other hand, then looks at Grandma Hamilton. "It was nice to see you again, Mrs. Hamilton," she says.

Grandma Hamilton smiles at her and nods.

Sasha and Dom run back to the stairs where their stuff was dumped. They grab it and hurry up to the platform, just missing the group. Chad's dad is waiting for them, "There you are," he says in a nice way, not like he is mad. "We'll have to wait for the next one."

Sasha and Dom stand quietly, and Sasha holds onto his hand and closes her eyes. This is a new trick the Prophets learned at camp. Sasha conjures up a thought and sends it to Stacy. Stacy can send and receive thoughts without eye contact. Sasha is asking for the names of the two Prophets they have not met yet. By holding Dom's hand, his job is to watch for anyone who may come up and wonder why Sasha has her eyes closed. This happened a bunch at camp when non-Prophet kids would interact with them. They had to find ways to communicate but not look suspicious. It was a bit embarrassing when one Prophet would call out another's name to get eye contact and "talk" to each other across a room full of people but not say anything out loud when attention was gained. They learned to get a third prophet to do the speaking out loud to cover for the eye contact communication. They did this a bunch during meals at camp.

"Xyril and Lilli," Sasha whispers to Dom as they wait for a train.

Dom nods in understanding mode.

"So how was camp?" Chad's dad asks.

Dom reacts as Sasha still has eyes closed. He lets her hand go as a sign that they are being watched. "It was fantastic. I especially liked the horse riding!" Dom says as if rehearsed.

Stacy gave all the Prophets instructions on how to respond to a question that would be asked over and over again: be positive and tell people one thing you really liked. The kids enjoyed all the regular parts of camp as usual. It was a new experience for Chad and Stacy, but there were lots of fun things to do. Mostly, the Prophets used every opportunity to practice communicating with each other within the groups of people around them at all times. At night they wouldn't get much sleep. They kept trying to dream-connect with each other. Everyone except Izaak; he would fall way too deep asleep and get real cranky if the dream wasn't important.

At the Lake Street stop, Dom and Sasha decide to drop off their stuff at home and meet at the treehouse in an hour. From there, they could see who is available to go meet the new Prophets. They decide that the boys should meet the male triplets and the girls can meet at Grandma Maxwell's house. The Prophets noticed that every time at camp they were in a boy-girl situation, other campers teased them as if they were boyfriend and girlfriend. They had become comfortable intermingling, but this seemed odd for typical ten-year-olds. They realized there were times to be together and times to be in same-gender groupings. They felt more adult and more mature, the more they embraced their Prophet identities. Other times, the boys would easily revert back to doing just boy stupid stuff. The girls were more solidly entrenched in this new maturity and felt slightly uncomfortable grouping with other girls. They all did surmise that Mr. Lazarus knew what he was doing by bringing them all together, and Sasha and Dom were eager to "tell" the others about Steve's news.

Izaak and Rich get to the first level of the treehouse just in time to hear Izzy remark out loud to Sasha and Dom, "*Triplets!* Crap, like I have enough to manage with my own sisters!"

"Hey guys, long time no see," Rich says, trying to be funny.

"Where is Cecilia?" Izzy asks Izaak.

"Out cold on the couch," He remarks, "Wu?"

She crawled into bed and keeps sending nonsense dreams to Stacy," Izzy reports.

The Stones's and Simms's have family in from the Lakotas.

"Any news on Zoltar?" Rich asks.

"I went by his place right away, but only chickens squacking at me when I knocked on the door," Dom reports dejectedly.

"'Squacking,' what the hell is that?" Izaak asks in fright. His imagination going wild with chickens flapping and jumping all around his head. Izaak doesn't like chickens.

"Clucking and squawking at the same time. I learned it at camp," Dom says with bizarre authority

"Bull crap," Izaak responds.

"OK, just us five; we can do this," Sasha interrupts the boys like a good leader reassuring a tired crew of Prophets.

"Yes!" Dom says, with energy.

"OK, here's the plan," Sasha begins. "Izaak, Rich, and Dom go meet the triplets at Mr. Fremont's old house. Dom, you find a window to look across the street to me, so we can talk. Izzy, you lead the conversation with Lilli."

"The new guy's name is Xyril, with an X?" Izaak asks.

"Yeah, different, huh?" Sasha says with a smile.

"Just like us," Rich says proudly.

They climb down to the ground and prepare themselves for the short journey across the block to the houses on the corners. The Dream Prophets have all taken on this identity in full seriousness. Wu is still apprehensive but is a sponge for learning and adventuring. Each of these five have some anxiousness, wishing all nine of them were together to meet the next two. Rich immensely missed Zoltar. He even tried sending him dream thoughts at night from camp, but he got no response.

"Isn't it kind of cool that we know these people will be our friends before we even meet them?" Rich says out loud what each of the other four were also thinking.

"Yeah, it's like at the end of that Casablanca film," Izzy says as they walk.

The boys look at each other, dumbfounded.

The boys get to the blue house, No. 2103 and the small porch steps. Dom looks over to Sasha at Grandma Maxwell's house. They synchronize their doorbell ringing.

Grandma Maxwell answers quickly. "Hello ladies, enjoying the evening cool?"

"Yes, maam," the two girls chime in quickly.

"We understand there is a new person here!" Sasha says in her best future teacher voice.

"Yes, maam, Xyril is at the piano playing lovely songs for his grandma!" she says very proudly.

The girls look at each other and share in their heads, *Xyril! Oh crap.*

They start to walk in. Sasha quickly positions herself in a window facing the blue house across the street.

Rich is on the top step as he rings the bell. There is no response. Dom has not caught the vibe yet to turn around. Rich rings the bell again. The door is pulled opened harshly and a very big man in a sweaty tank top with a military buzz cut answers. The boys immediately notice his prickly chest hair peeking out at them menacingly. The man has a scowl, then rights himself at the sight of three harmless boys.

"We came to see Xyril," Rich says.

"and his brothers," Izaak adds quickly.

The man is very puzzled. "Nobody here by that name," and he closes the door.

The boys don't know what to do.

Dom turns around and looks over to Grandma Maxwell's house. He finds Sasha in the window waving her hands like Steve Hamilton with an ice cream cone. They connect eyes.

"Oh crap," Dom says out loud and turns to the other guys.

Before he can speak, the blue door opens up again. This time a small, skinny, bald-headed girl opens the door.

"Hello," she says with a full touch of chipper in her voice.

"Lilli!" Dom says out loud.

Izaak and Rich look at each other, and in their heads, exclaim *oh crap.*

"Do I know you? Lilli says happily. "Ya'll wanna come in for lemonade. I just made a pitcher, You like my head?" She says rubbing her shocking baldness. "I just did it, well actually my brothers did it. They wanted to see how low the setting would go on the clippers. I know it's different. I don't have cancer; I just wanted to try something new!" Lilli says all of this in one breath as she leads the boys into the house and into the dining room.

Dexter and Ian Lazlo are in the dining room, trying to stay out of the way. Their hair is short and in a buzz cut like the man who first answered. Lilli's hair is down to the nub and noticeably shorter. Boxes and boxes of stuff are still unpacked. The boys are sitting across from the boys who walk in, looking as if their whole original plan has been shot to hell.

Sasha stays close to the window. Grandma Maxwell has led the girls into the house. They see Xyril with his long black Lakota braids sitting with his back to them at the piano. He is playing very slow, finishing up a song just for his grandma. He seems to have been oblivious to the doorbell and Grandma even having been gone. He finishes and immediately says, "Hey, Grandma, here is some stuff I have been working on," and he starts to play something upbeat. "I have been listening to my new ELP album, and I just about got this one song figured out. He starts playing "Hoedown."

The girls remain quiet. They are following Grandma Maxwell's lead and wait for an introduction.

"Here's the lemonade," Lilli says. She has a big pitcher and a stack of cups. "Let's go out front and sit on the porch. Mom and Dad are fried from unpacking. Dexter and Ian get up and realize they have company. They follow their sister as she leads everybody out to the front porch.

Xyril plays quite well until he gets stuck. He tries to fix his mistake and gets stuck again.

BOGART E. NOMAD | 111

"Son of a shit crapper!" he says out loud and whirls around to see Grandma with the girls.

He turns beat red with embarrassment"

"Xryril, dear, we have company," Grandma says calmly.

"Hi," Sasha says to break the awkwardness. "We are the welcoming committee for this block. My name is Sasha, and this is Izzabella,"

Izzy gives her a look of displeasure at hearing her full name revealed.

Xyril nods and turns back around to play but changes his mind and gets up and bows to the girls and heads back into another part of the house.

They hear a door close with a solid but gentle click.

Grandma motions over to the couch for the girls to sit.

They settle in on a very plush golden-colored couch.

"Xyril is in pain," she begins as if telling a story. "Xyril came to me damaged but hopeful." She continues, "He is an only child, and his parents are recently departed."

The girls gasp and realize the sound may be sudden.

"It's all right, ladies. I am actually hoping you and the other neighborhood kids can help us out. It will take time, but Xyril will need new friends. It's just him and me now. "

"What happened," Sasha asks respectfully

"Car crash."

Izzy holds out her hand to Miss Maxwell. Sasha looks to the window.

The girls are not sure what to say.

Grandma Maxwell lets the pause of silence run its natural course, then says before the girls can form a new thought, "I will make sure he meets with all of you all on Sunday at noon with Mr. Lazarus."

The girls look at her directly. She smiles and turns away before a thought can be shared.

The two girls walk out of the house and see the group across the way drinking lemonade on the porch steps. They walk over.

Lilli spots them and hops up quickly, "More lemonade—we need more lemonade!" and runs into the house. "Talk among yourselves! Here's a topic: what's your favorite body part?"

Sasha and Izzy sit on the sidewalk in front of the boys.

"My hands," Dexter says out loud but carefully. "I am a pitcher, a lefty." This breaks the ice. The other boys chime in with baseball chatter. The girls look at each and share a thought to each other: *This will be OK.*

Lilli comes back and is a perfect host, pouring lemonade and bopping Ian on the head when he reaches for a cookie from the plate she brought out. "Guests first," she says without missing a beat.

"I am quite fond of my uvula! If it wasn't there I might not be able to swallow properly. You see, I talk while I eat too much and I could choke if my uvula didn't work as well as it does." She finishes handing out cups and cookies and sits down next to the girls. She sits just close enough to make eye contact with both of them. The boys have continued with their baseball talk, sharing little league tales of conquest and runs and tag outs and how Zoltar is their best player, but he isn't here just now.

Lilli focuses back on her eye contact with Sasha and Izzy. She takes a big swig of sweetness. Closes her eyes and sends a glance very forcefully to the girls eyes. *We meet Mr. Lazarus on Sunday.*

The girls smile and realize what Lilli has done. They all three giggle with glee.

Lilli gives the boys a few more moments. They could talk about baseball all day. She interjects during a lull in the conversation.

"OK, now the topic is Dreams. Who wants to share?"

Rich spews his lemonade all over Dom.

Sunday morning blooms like a breezy petal dislodged from a tired rose. Most of the Prophets are asleep. It's 8:15 a.m., and Big Willy has started his countdown. Xyril has it on low, the big stereo his dad left behind tuned into Big Willy's show. He does not want to wake up his grandma. He is in his room, the big room on the second floor overlooking the front porch and the archway that takes up most of the lawn. Grandma told him the history of it, but he doesn't remember all of it. He is feeling lonely. He only has his KTOE tuned in, hoping that the DJ will play an Emerson, Lake, and Palmer song. His French doors are open, catching the morning spirit wind. He thinks about going onto the porch, when he sees a young girl walk up and sit on the archway. He can see her profile. She hops up onto the ledge and kicks her legs back and forth. *She is beautiful,* he thinks to himself. It is Jaydici. She abruptly turns her head and looks behind her. Dom is walking up to greet her.

"Hello, Miss Jade!" Dom exclaims and sits up next to her. They do not know Xyril is watching.

"Hey," she says and slumps her shoulders forward.

"It's the brothers again, isn't it?" Dom says and lifts her head up a bit to make eye contact. "Which brother was it this time?" Dom asks.

"All seven of them," she blurts out and starts to cry.

Xyril can see what's going on but can only read the body language. He feels something at his leg. Boozu Bones, the tomcat, is rubbing up against his leg and purring. He looks up at Xyril to get his attention. He then walks up to the open door and looks to the left, out the open space, inviting Xyril to join him. Xyril scooches his chair up quietly. He doesn't want Dom and Jaydici to see him spying on them. He looks to where Boozu is pointing with his purring. He sees the new neighbor, Lilli, walking very quietly toward the treehouse. She looks over to the archway and appears to be sneaking away from her house, not wanting to be noticed by Dom and Jaydici.

Lilli is headed to the treehouse to meet up with Tulpen who flew in last night with her five kittens. Xyril doesn't know this yet, but Grandma does. Boozu Bones the gray, white, and black cat is the Father.

Lilli tiptoes quietly and is not detected. She makes her way to the base of the tree. She starts to climb when she hears someone up above. Wu is in the treehouse with Tulpen and her kittens.

Lilli hesitates briefly but has felt a strong urge to be here at this moment, directed by a dream she just had ten minutes ago. It woke her up and directed her. She pokes her head into the landing of the first level.

"Hello," she whispers. She is much calmer than she was when she was hosting the boys on Friday afternoon with lemonade.

"Hello. You must be Lilli," Wu says very calmly. She has a bright green girl kitty and a bright lilac girl kitty in her lap. The kitties are very awake and playful this morning. Lilli surveys the scene. There is a bright orange male and a cobalt electric blue male kitty wrestling in the corner. The sunshine yellow female is trying to pester Tulpen to play. Tulpen is on the opposite side from the opening curled up next to Tabitha, Stacy's black-and-purple feline. Tulpen is tired from the morning. The kitties are weened but still very needy. Lilli pauses to watch but not disturb. The orange and blue toms stop wrestling and bolt toward the opening to Lilli. She crawls up quickly and sits cross-legged, blocking the opening. The toms jump onto her and continue to wrestle, using Lilli as a mat.

Back at the archway; Dom has his left arm around Jaydici's shoulders, and she has almost finished her big cry.

"Let it all out," he says to her as he holds her. Her body heaves up and down, letting out weeks up pent-up emotion.

Xyril feels an urge to leave his loneliness and do something bold. This would be a new thing for him. He has, up until now, a shy personality. He looks to Boozu.

"Should I go down and introduce myself?" He asks his new family member.

Boozu continues to purr, watching the treehouse like a hawk.

"I should ... I can be more outgoing," He says to Boozu without response.

"I can buck up and be a *man;* I can take care of myself and Grandma," he says with whispered authority to himself and an unflinching Boozu.

Xyril gets up and stands tall. Boozu turns and looks to him and calmly winks a long slow gesture with his left eye. He turns back and refocuses on the treehouse.

Xyril turns, shuts off his big stereo, and heads downstairs.

Wu and Lilli are very quiet and content to let the kittens play on them. The gentle summer breeze blows through the treehouse window with a cool morning rush. Lilli breaks the silence.

"What is your name again?" she asks respectfully

"I am Wu Punabi," she says with a smile. "Welcome to Mistletoe!"

Lilli smiles and concentrates on petting both tom boy kitties in her lap at once.

"Where are ya'll from?" Wu asks while one kitty hangs from her slightly outstretched arm.

Lilli sighs and gathers her story, "We just moved here from Galveston, Texas, but we were only there for four months. We didn't even get fully unpacked. Before Galveston, we were from our home in New York City. I really miss New York."

Wu ponders for a bit, then asks, "What do you miss most?"

"Bagels and Yoo Hoo," Lilli says without hesitation.

"Wu Who?" Wu asks?

Lilli laughs out loud in her usual volume of voice. "No, YOOHOO. It's like a chocolate milk drink, very popular in New York. I haven't seen it in Texas yet."

"Oh, I see," Wu says then gets an idea

"I bet Pinky can get it for you at her store" Wu says raising her voice a bit. All seven cats have now stopped playing and are watching the two humans conversing.

"Well! Pinky is my new second best new friend!" Lilli says with glee.

"Second best?" Wu takes the bait.

"Yes, I, Lilli Linda Lu Lazlo has declared that you, Wu Punabi, is my first new best friend fellow cat lover"

Wu sits up straight and smiles and then turns to make eye contact with Lilli, "Did you say Linda Lou was your middle name?"

Lilli read her thought from her eyes.

"Lu with an L U , not Lou" she sends that thought to Wu without speaking.

Wu smiles and looks at Tulpen. Tulpen winks at her with assured approval, that yes, Lilli is also a Dream Prophet.

Wu reconnects eye contact with Lilli, "My middle name is Lu also, Wu Lu Punabi!" she sends this thought to Lilli.

"I am gonna like it here!" Lilli speaks aloud and raises the cobalt blue tom kitty up high above her head with outstretched arms. The kitty howls with the happiness of a wolf in full moonlight.

Xyril has opened his front door and walked out onto his porch for Dom and Jaydici to see him. He confidently walks down to the archway bench and stands in front of the two of them. He puts his arms behind him and declares, "I am Xyril B. Homecoming, and I am new to this town."

Dom hops down and faces him with an outstretched hand. "My name is Dom, and this is Jaydici."

They shake hands and properly meet, in an official manner.

Jaydici raises a hand and half waves at Xyril. It is only a bit awkward. Xyril knows she has been crying but decides to stay on task.

"I just moved here about a week or so ago, I am from Akron, Iowa, originally by way of the Lakota territory." He sways back and forth a bit as he talks but still remains confident that he has made a good decision to meet them.

"Grandma Maxwell told us about you, a bit" Dom says choosing his words carefully.

Dom would later realize that he was showing some rudimentary but genuine chaplain skills in this moment. He was helping Jaydici and Xyril at the same time by being a conscious presence with both of them. Dom continues, "You have a unique name. It's almost as cool as mine."

Xyril smiles.

"It's Xyril with an "X"? How cool is that?" Dom says hoping for a story.

"Yes! My dad legally changed our family last name to Homecoming. He did this not long after I was born. He was briefly home from Viet Nam. I was born while he was away, and they messed up the spelling. I was supposed to be Cyril with a "C," like my dad's brother's name. His brother Cyril died in Viet Nam. My mom thought it was spelled with an "X." I was born a Maxwell, but dad was so happy to be home, he wanted to rename our family the Homecomings. But when he filled out the paperwork and spent all the money to change it, he forgot to change the "X." My dad was a bit forgetful."

Reflective pause.

"What's the "B" stand for?" Dom asks

"It's just a "B" short for, We will *be* coming home, I think. I may have to ask Grandma about that one."

"Your dad sounds," Dom pauses for the right word, "interesting"

"Yes, Grandma called him a character when she was happy with him and a fool when he did something stupid."

Dom senses a bit of sadness and invites Xyril to join them in sitting on the Archway bench. Jaydici pats the open spot next to her.

They all three sit and look forward onto Lake street. Bluford Foot is waving at them cordially and headed out with his milk cart.

Xyril breaks the silence, "My mom and dad died in a car crash three weeks ago today." He says this as though it is the first time he has actually acknowledged that it happened.

Jaydici places her right hand on Xyril's left hand very gently for re-assurance. She left all her tears on Dom, and now she has some strength for someone else.

"They don't allow cars in Mistletoe," she says with full sincerity.

Xyril looks at her with a thankful smile.

The kittens are settling down a bit, and Wu speaks up.

"Hey, Lilli, I feel a need to ask," she says hopefully.

Lilli is sitting comfortably with her back to the wall of the treehouse.

"Yeah?" she replies.

"What is with the hair?" She raises up the green kitty pretending that the kitty asked the question.

Lilli smiles big and takes in a deep breath, looking up to the roof for an answer.

"I don't really know why I did it. Maybe to be like my brothers; they always get really short buzz cuts for summer in the heat. And it is really hot in Texas! It was a quick decision, but maybe on a deeper level, I wanted a fresh start to this new life here in Mistletoe. I do *not* want to move again, and I really, really hope my parents can get along better," she pauses at the thought of oversharing. Wu sits listening with all her attention.

"Mostly, I really wanted to feel my head!" Lilli continues. "I like rubbing my brothers' heads when they are buzzed. It feels all prickly and fuzzy at the same time. I wanted to feel that for myself. My hair was all thick and long, and I was sick of it anyway."

Wu takes it all in. "Cool," she says calmly as the lilac kitty falls asleep in her lap with the yellow one. "Very cool"

Wu takes in the moment and then gets a rush of information in her head.

Lilli seems to notice this but remains quiet.

"Hey, Lu" Wu says playfully, "We have been given a job."

"Yes, Lu!" Lilli says and waits for a directive.

"The kitties are ready to be transported to their new homes. "Wu adjusts her legs and gets up, disturbing the lap full of purr.

She stands and looks at the group of kitties who are now all looking at her as if she is their mother now.

"Lilli, you get to take the yellow one home to the Lazlo house. Xyril, your neighbor across from your house gets the blue one." Lilli collects the two kitties.

"I will take the orange one to the Black family next door." Wu ends her directives.

"What about the Green and Lilac ones?" Lilli asks.

"I will care for them until further instructed," Wu says with distinct maturity.

Grandma Maxwell is now sitting on her porch with Boozu Bones in her lap. The three new friends on the archway bench look over at the new distraction.

Xyril speaks up, "Hey I wonder what number Big Willy is at by now?"

What time is it?" Jaydici asks.

"It's 9:37," Grandma Maxwell says without looking at any watch or timepiece.

"I didn't bring my transistor with me," Dom remarks.

"I got a *big* stereo in my room; we can listen there if you want," Xyril says very happily.

He looks over to his grandma, "Ya'll come on in. I got gravy on the stove and biscuits in the oven."

Dom jumps down right away. He knows about that gravy.

The three head upstairs to Xyril's room. He turns on the stereo.

That was No. 24, "Dixie Chicken," a song by Big Willy's favorite new band, Little Feat. Big Willy had never heard of Little Feat before. They spell Feat with an A, like they are the Beatles, or something. They already have three albums out and I never heard of them before. Big Willy must be slipping! The boss lady may grumble at me later, but Big Willy is gonna play another Little Feat song. Yes, you heard me, back to back! There is crowd noises of approval from the people gathered at his booth.

This one is from their second album, Easy to Slip—No. 23!

Xyril looks to Dom with a quizzical look.

"Big Willy is a totally cool cat," Dom says.

Dom is eyeballing Xyril's record collection. Jaydici has plopped onto the couch in the corner and is petting Boozu at her feet. Boozu is very curious with all this new commotion in his house.

"Who's your favorite band?" Dom asks secretly hoping to look through Xyril's albums.

"Oh yeah," Xyril was distracted while watching Jaydici and Boozu. "Uuhmm, mostly the usual bands … Beatles, Byrds, Bob Dylan, and the Who, but right now I am very excited about Emerson, Lake, and Palmer. You know, ever since I got serious about playing the piano."

Jaydici perks up, "Wanna hear one of their songs on the radio?"

"Sure!" Xyril says very happily

Jaydici looks around, "Where's your phone?"

"Out in the hall," Xyril turns and points. Jaydici scampers to make a call.

Dom and Xyril strain their ears to listen.

"Hey, Pinky, it's Jaydici!" she turns on the little girl cheery charm. "Hey, can I get in a new-resident request? Yeah! I know, No. 20 is coming up soon. OK, oh, yeah, something by a band called Emerson, Lake, and Peter!"

"Palmer," Xyril calls out.

"Palmer! Sorry, have you heard of them? It's for a cute guy named Xyril with an X."

Xyril blushes but only Dom can see.

Jaydici walks back to the stereo and sits waiting to hear of her accomplishment. She is proud of herself.

Lilli has come down from the treehouse with the blue kitty held close to her chest. The yellow kitty is sitting perfectly content on Lilli's shoulder. She is headed to Grandma Maxwell's house. She walks up the steps to the porch. She hears a stern meow from up above. Boozu is meowing with proud approval. Lilli sits down in the chair next to Grandma Maxwell.

"I have been instructed to bring this kitty to Xyril," Lilli says to Grandma. Grandma Maxwell is happy to receive the blue ball of fur. She hands Lilli the Sunday Comix, "Trade ya!"

"Oh, my lord, how beautiful this little man!" Grandma exclaims. She places the kitty in her lap, and he instinctually lays out flat across her legs and purrs himself to closed eyes and contentment.

Lilli watches and then opens the comix to find her favorite strip, Blondie with Dagwood Bumstead, the perfect dad.

Grandma pets the kitty for a good long while until Boozu climbs down from the balcony. He places himself between the two humans and sits up straight like a furry Dagwood. He winks at his daughter wrapped around Lilli's neck.

"Will you stay for breakfast?" Grandma asks sweetly.

Lilli closes the comix section, "I must pass this time; my family is probably awake and I am in charge of eggs this morning!"

"You scooch on home, child! You can make eggs with me next time." Grandma sends her on her way.

Upstairs the radio is turned up loud. Xyril waits for his favorite new band to welcome him into the community of Mistletoe. The three new friends head downstairs to the smell of the best gravy this side of New Orleans.

Blufoot enters the block with his cart. His transistor breaks the Sunday morning silence.

OK, KTOE people, we have reached No. 20, and we have a request! This goes out to a new Mistletoe transplant. Please welcome Xyril with an "X." You are now part of the KTOE community! Here is Emerson, Lake, and Palmer from England with a song called "The Sheriff." Enjoy!

Almost Noon:

At the Hamilton house, on the fifth floor, at the tippy top of the stairs, Steve, Ringo, and Cecilia are jamming for the first time. Steve has invited the ladies and their guitars to use the empty room in the back side of the house, where they can play as loud as they want. The open window overlooks the backyard and the Black Family deck where the meeting with Mr. Lazarus will soon commence. Ringo brought a two-headed bongo for Steve to bong on. Turns out, Steve keeps pretty good rhythm, and he mentions at least five times in this past hour how much he wants to get a drum set.

Rich and Izaak are already on the deck waiting for the others. They can hear the music above them. They are quite amused by the antics of the bright orange tom cat kitty that Wu has bestowed onto the Black family. They have an old fishing rod with a balled-up piece of yarn on the end that was endless fun for the orange kitty. Mr. Black is crashed out on the couch in his garage shed watching a baseball game with his eyes closed. The boys left the volume up loud enough to drown out the meeting.

Dom and Sasha are walking to the Maxwell house to invite Xyril out to "play." No need for a ruse; Grandma Maxwell always seems to know what is going on with the Prophets.

"I got lots of questions for Mr. Lazarus; let me tell you" he says to Sasha half complaining.

"I get this necklace with hardly *any* explanation of what it does," he continues.

Sasha nods and ignores his rant in the same movement.

"It's not always about you," she says under her breath.

Wu and Izzy stop by Lilli's house and collect her officially so her parents know where she will be. She takes the yellow kitty from her neck and places it in the large planter on the porch. It curls up for a nap as if told to do so.

Chad and Stacy leave the Lake Street Diner and cut through Stacy's backyard and are the last to arrive just as Cecilia is coming out of Steve's back door.

Mr. Lazarus walks up, looking confused.

Izaak sees him first and waves to him, "Hello, Mr. Lazarus!"

Mr. Lazarus doesn't acknowledge his wave. He walks up the steps of the deck and finds a spot on the end of the table. He sets down the old chest that he had last time they were all together.

The Prophets quiet down and sit around the two big picnic tables that Mr. Black has placed out for the larger group. It is a bit of a tight fit, but everyone is sitting comfortably. Mr. Lazarus is at the head of the table.

"I thought we would be at the other spot by the treehouse?" He says sounding a bit perturbed.

"We thought this spot would be better with more shade," Izaak states.

Just then the guitar and bongo playing becomes lively and not quite muffled enough for Mr. Lazarus's taste. He looks up to the window across the Hamilton's backyard. The window slowly closes and the sound diminishes.

Mr. Lazarus ponders the logic of Izaak's statement. He agrees with the sentiment. He closes his eyes and calms his nerves. He does not send out this thought. He does not want to alarm the youth. He has lost track of Zoltar recently, and he doesn't want to delay the schedule he has for the Prophets any longer. *Eleven out of Twelve ain't bad for now,* is his final thought before opening his eyes.

He scans the crowd. Everyone looks attentive. They are ready for answers and discovering totems for the two new people. He makes eye contact with each Prophet. When he gets to Lilli, she has a slightly angry look on her face. She sends him a thought, *Where is Zoltar, and why is he missing?*

How did you do that? he sends a thought back.

She looks away and turns her eyes onto the orange cat playing on the table in front of her.

Mr. Lazarus recollects his thoughts to focus on the tasks at hand.

"Hello, to all of you," he states in his teacher voice.

Each of the Prophets send a greeting to him in their own way.

"I want to especially welcome our new arrivals. Xyril and Lilli, welcome to Mistletoe and the Dream Prophets" Mr. Lazarus says and extends his arms to include everybody.

Xyril raises his hand.

"Mr. Homecoming, yes, a question" Mr. Lazarus is pointing to Xyril.

"Uhhmm, what's a Dream Prophet?" He asks very curiously.

Mr. Lazarus looks straight at Stacy, then over to Sasha, then Dom and finally Lilli. He gets no answers from any of them.

He looks back at Xyril. Xyril has a totally blank look on his face and in his mind.

"Mr. Homecoming, are you saying that you are not clear as to why you are here with this group of people?" Mr. Lazarus's face turns beet red with anxiety.

Xyril remains quiet with the most quizzical look on his face that he can muster. He looks around the table to the others. They avoid his eyes. He redirects his gaze to Mr. Lazarus. Then he slowly smiles the biggest grin he can manage without laughing.

"Just foolin' with ya, Mr. Lazarus," he reveals. He looks deep into Mr. Lazarus's eyes and sends a message, *Grandmama says hi.*

Izaak laughs first, "Good one! Oh, he got ya good, Mr. Lazarus!"

Mr. Lazarus feels his heart skip a beat. He lets go of his deep breath and smiles as big as Izaak. He remembers now why he picked these eleven fine young boys and girls. He wishes he knew where Zoltar was to complete the group.

The group settles down and gives the floor back to Mr. Lazarus.

"OK then, we have a few totems to deliver."

"Xryli B. Homecoming" he says properly.

He opens the trunk and reaches in and pulls out a large coin that has been cut in half with a zigzag cut.

"This is a Mizpah coin. Well, half of a Mizpah coin. It is the first one ever made. Its purpose will be made clear to you at a much later date. For now," he pauses for effect, "your main skill will be as a listener, a romantic, and a theologian. You will be a writer and a preacher." He hands the half coin to Xyril. Before he releases it to Xyril, he adds. " Keep playing the piano and keep being a smart ass."

The group erupts in laughter.

This brings us to Lilli Linda Lu Lazlo.

He reaches in and brings out an old-looking reflex hammer that doctors use. He hands it to Lilli.

"You are a healer. All living creatures, human, animal and otherwise are yours to care for both physically and psychologically. This totem is the first-ever reflex hammer. Your identity is to continue to study in the medical field using your natural talents. It appears you also have a talent I did not know about." Mr. Lazarus looks directly into Lilli's eyes and raises his own eyebrow for effect.

Lilli freezes with the hammer in her hand. She looks around the table. She appears that she is about to burst with a secret to share.

"I am a clairvoyant," she says with a burst of exuberance. She puts her hands on the table and lets out a big breath of something she has been holding onto for a long time.

"Wow!, it feels good to get that off my chest" she looks around at stunned and quizzical faces.

"Clare who?" Dom asks

"She can read minds" Sasha says to Dom very teacher like but not as to embarrass him.

"Oh" Dom says, "But we all do that now, right"

"Lilli can read minds before you can send a thought" Stacy says and looks at Lilli with a bit of jealousy.

"Thank you, Miss Lazlo, good to know," Mr. Lazarus takes over the conversation again.

"That brings us to the final piece of business we have today."

"Are you going to answer our questions?" Dom says quickly.

The table grows quieter and Mr. Lazarus senses a need of importance from the Prophets.

He pauses to collect his thoughts

"We are not all here. I would like to wait until Zoltar returns to address any questions," Mr. Lazarus states with a calculated ease of patience that he knows won't be received well. This reminds him of the last batch of Prophets he tried to train close to ten years ago.

"Where is Zoltar? I am getting very worried about him," Rich says loudly.

No one from his family is speaking about it. I don't speak Spanish, but I *know* not everybody at the Gomez family house can't speak English.

"He pauses realizing his grammar was messed up, but he is too emotional to care.

"I'm getting pretty frustrated over here" Rich's voice starts to quiver before shedding a tear.

They all look at Mr. Lazarus for answers.

He reaches into the chest for the final totem and

raises up a tattered black chord with a gold whistle at the end of it.

"Zoltar's totem is a whistle from the first Olympics." Mr. Lazarus hands the whistle to Rich. "As all you already know, Zoltar is great at sports, all sports. This will be his destiny, professionally. Within the group here, he will serve as the referee to any and all disputes, kind of like a judge."

"Why do I get the whistle?" Rich asks very cautiously not wanting the answer but compelled to ask for his dear friend.

Mr. Lazarus looks down at the table. His knees betray him, and he has to sit down.

"I am afraid that we have lost Zoltar," Mr. Lazarus states slowly.

"Lost! What does that mean?!" Rich says, tears streaming down his face.

"Tulpen and I have been tracking him out in California, with his family. They were working on the family vineyards in wine country." He

catches his breath. "There was some trouble one night, then we lost him."
Mr. Lazarus looks up to see the stunned faces.

Izzy puts her arms around Rich to console him. Cecilia notices that
Izaak is quietly sobbing as well.

"Trouble—like Mr. Fremont kind of trouble?" Sasha asks as leader of
the group.

Mr. Lazarus begins to explain more when a large commotion interrupts everyone's thoughts. It is coming from the path that leads from the
treehouse to the deck where they are sitting.

A huge Great Dane puppy comes loping up the trail and headed for
the table on the deck. With one great leap, the big pup hops up scattering
the Prophets and heads for the orange kitty who is sleeping in front of
Cecilia by Mr. Lazarus. The cat doesn't flinch. The dog is pointing at the
cat like it has been hunting all day for it. His large tail wagging knocks
the hat clean off of Dom's head.

Lilli makes a sound, the dog turns to look at her. He whimpers and
sits immediately.

Then a loud yell comes from the path where the dog had emerged.

"Cabesa De Vaca! Pendejo!" a loud voice yells. This is followed by the
sound of the dirt and gravel being disturbed on the path.

"Zoltar?" Rich says loudly.

A large Mexican boy walks up to the group.

The table is stunned. Mr. Lazarus is relieved.

"Que pasa, ya'll!" Zoltar walks up and stands at the end of the table
opposite Mr. Lazarus.

"What did I miss?"

Printed in the USA
CPSIA information can be obtained
at www.ICGtesting.com
LVHW041459031023
760013LV00001B/2